"Liberty, if I kiss you now, I won't be able to stop," Finn said.

"I want you, Finn," she murmured, her eyes never leaving his.

Finn kissed the pale, soft skin of her shoulder, then seared her delicate throat with his yearning mouth. "You're beautiful, Liberty, like ivory velvet." His voice was harsh with passion and need.

Liberty splayed one hand on Finn's back, feeling his muscles tense and move beneath his clothes. She sank the fingers of her other hand into his thick, blond hair, reveling in the touch of his mouth on hers.

Finn's hands moved over her body, covered by the thin fabric of her sundress, and her blood hummed through her veins like liquid fire.

An artist's hands, she thought dreamily. Hands that created beauty on canvas and made her feel beautiful by their mere touch. It was as though he were painting her image in his mind as he caressed her. . . .

WHAT ARE *LOVESWEPT* ROMANCES?

They are stories of true romance and touching emotion. We believe those two very important ingredients are constants in our highly sensual and very believable stories in the *LOVESWEPT* line. Our goal is to give you, the reader, stories of consistently high quality that may sometimes make you laugh, sometimes make you cry, but are always fresh and creative and contain many delightful surprises within their pages.

Most romance fans read an enormous number of books. Those they truly love, they keep. Others may be traded with friends and soon forgotten. We hope that each *LOVESWEPT* romance will be a treasure—a "keeper." We will always try to publish

LOVE STORIES YOU'LL NEVER FORGET
BY AUTHORS YOU'LL ALWAYS REMEMBER

The Editors

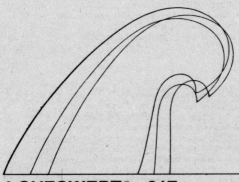

LOVESWEPT® • 317

Joan Elliott Pickart
Riddles and Rhymes

BANTAM BOOKS
TORONTO • NEW YORK • LONDON • SYDNEY • AUCKLAND

RIDDLES AND RHYMES

A Bantam Book / March 1989

If you would be interested in receiving protective vinyl covers for your Loveswept books, please write to this address for information:

Loveswept
Bantam Books
P.O. Box 985
Hicksville, NY 11802

ISBN 0-553-21966-9

Published simultaneously in the United States and Canada

PRINTED IN THE UNITED STATES OF AMERICA

O   0 9 8 7 6 5 4 3 2 1

For Beverly Sauer

One

The man was watching her again.

Liberty Shaw stood in the dark living room and peered through the drapes. A chill swept over her as she saw him in the shadows across the street. From her vantage point in the second floor apartment, there was no doubt in her mind that he was looking up at her, just as he'd done the night before.

She couldn't see his features clearly. She only knew he was short and stocky, was dressed in dark clothes, and was watching her.

She pulled the drapes tightly together and crossed her arms over her body, wrapping her hands around her elbows in a protective gesture. She stared at the drapes, irrationally thinking that they were all that stood between her and the man who was turning her blood to ice.

She was being absurd, she told herself, making a big deal out of nothing. For all she knew, the man was simply following his nightly routine of going for a walk, then stopping for a while to enjoy the cool early summer air. This was only her second night in the apartment, and she had no plausible reason to believe he'd shown up for the purpose of watching her.

But his head was tilted back in such a way that she knew he was looking at *her* windows!

"Oh, Liberty, stop it," she said aloud.

She spun around and turned on the lamp on one end table, then on the other, lighting the cluttered room. Her gaze swept across the small expanse, the man in the shadows momentarily forgotten as she looked at the seemingly endless number of boxes filled with books. The shabby furniture appeared to have been added as an afterthought, a necessary nuisance taking up space that could have been better used for books.

Liberty wove her way around and over the boxes to reach the minuscule kitchen. She made herself a salad and a ham sandwich for dinner. As she sat down at the small Formica-topped table to eat, her thoughts were pulled once more to the man standing below in the shadows.

No, she thought, she wasn't going to scare herself silly over what was nothing more than an innocent act by someone who had been in the neighborhood much longer than she had. She would put her mental energies to much better use by deciding what on earth she was going to do with this place she'd inherited from an aunt she hardly knew.

The cluttered apartment, she thought dryly, was

neat as a pin compared to the bookstore directly below. Used books filled the shelves to overflowing, the excess stacked in piles here, there, and everywhere. It was a dusty, musty mess, and it was hers. She loved books. They had been her best friends when she'd been growing up. Her father's army career had required her family to move often, and she'd sought solace in books when she was once again the new girl in school, alone and lonely.

Yes, she loved books, but to have suddenly inherited what seemed to be a zillion of them, along with the small store and apartment above it, was a tad overwhelming. But she was there, and she'd make the best of the situation. She had the entire summer at her disposal. That was one of the perks of being a schoolteacher, as long as a person could figure out how not to starve to death on the small paycheck that went with the job. Taking on the challenge of The Book Mark, her aunt's used book store, was certainly different from the various occupations she'd had during the summer hiatus in the past.

The Book Mark, she repeated silently. She liked the name—as much as people had liked her aunt Beverly. Liberty had arrived late yesterday and had done little more than see the attorney, buy some groceries, flick away the layer of dust in the apartment, then head for bed. Today she'd propped the door of the store open with the hope of airing out the place. It had been closed for the two weeks since her aunt's death.

People had started arriving almost immediately,

delighted that The Book Mark was once more open for business. Each and every person had asked who Liberty was, then expressed their sympathy, as well as their own sense of loss over the death of their friend Bev Shaw.

Liberty had been gracious but quiet, not wishing to admit she'd only met her aunt once when she was ten years old. She could remember vivid fragments about the small woman: a swishing fuchsia-colored shawl, numerous necklaces of bright beads, a clanking row of bracelets on one arm, and a delightful laugh that had sounded to Liberty like wind chimes on a breezy day.

She knew little about her aunt Beverly. She had been her father's older sister and was, from the snatches of things Colonel Shaw had said, the black sheep of the family. "Her behavior is disgraceful," her father had once roared in disgust. The colonel had not even personally informed Liberty of her aunt's death. He'd instructed Liberty's mother to include the news in the weekly letter from Germany, where her parents were presently stationed.

Liberty had been saddened when she realized no family members would be present at Aunt Beverly's funeral. Black sheep or not, she was still a Shaw. Then she'd received the certified letter from an attorney in Los Angeles informing her that she'd inherited The Book Mark from her aunt.

The letter, unbelievably, had come on the last day of the school year, and two days later Liberty had boarded a plane in Chicago, heading for L.A.

Yesterday she'd seen the attorney, been given

the keys to the store and apartment, signed the necessary papers, and that was that. She was now the official owner of a cluttered bookstore and shabby apartment in a run-down section of L.A. It was a wonder, she thought, inwardly laughing, that she couldn't hear her father bellowing all the way from Germany.

Liberty washed the few dishes she'd used, then headed for the tiny bathroom to take a shower. Even the little time she'd had between customers to explore the store had resulted in her becoming coated with dust, just like the books. If she sold the store, she would have to clean it thoroughly first to make it more appealing to a prospective buyer.

If she sold the store? she asked herself, standing under the soothing spray of water. Of course she was going to sell it. Wasn't she? Granted, she'd been counting the days, hours, and minutes until the final bell rang on the last day of school. That was a normal reaction, though, to ending a long and tedious school year of trying to teach English Literature to high school seniors who couldn't care less.

But, she admitted, this school year had seemed especially grim, and her social life a dull routine. She'd somehow fallen into the pattern of seeing Fred Newton, the computer science teacher, every Saturday night. Fred was hinting that it was time they had a serious discussion regarding their future, and had been none too pleased when she told him she was leaving for the summer. She'd felt a rush of relief that she could postpone the gruesome task of telling Fred she considered him nothing more than pleasant company and a good friend.

In short, Liberty mused, as she dried herself with a zebra-striped towel she'd found in a cupboard, her life had been boring. Dull, drab, and boring. Well, not anymore. At the moment, she owned a crummy little bookstore covered in dust. Not as exciting as a trip to Hawaii, or the Bahamas, or wherever, but most definitely a change. And Liberty Shaw was, indeed, ready for a change.

She pulled on a cotton nightshirt that came to mid-thigh and had a silk-screened picture of Shakespeare's face on the front. In the living room she checked the lock on the door and turned out the lights. She'd read in bed, she decided, until she felt ready to fall asleep.

Halfway to the bedroom, she stopped in the now dark living room, her gaze drawn to the curtained window.

No, she told herself, she was not going to look out that window again. Oh, darn it, yes, she was.

She waited until her eyes adjusted to the darkness, then cautiously walked toward the window, picturing broken toes and bruised shins as she wove through the obstacle course of boxes. At the window she took a steadying breath, opened the drapes a crack and peered through. A soft gasp escaped from her lips and her heart thudded wildly as she stared down into the shadows across the street.

He was still there.

And he was watching her.

• • •

Finn O'Casey left the small cafe that smelled like stale grease and provided, in his opinion, the best breakfast anywhere, and strolled leisurely along the sidewalk. He was miles and a culture apart from his sprawling home in Beverly Hills, and it felt great.

He glanced around as he walked. The crumbling buildings along the street housed small businesses, with cramped apartments above the stores. Trash littered the sidewalk, and a mangy dog was busily sniffing a pile. A baby cried somewhere in the distance; a woman leaned out of an upstairs window and yelled for Louie to get his butt home right that minute; a wino slept in the doorway of a boarded-up store, a brown paper bag clutched to his chest.

It was seedy, rank, and, to Finn, earthy and real. Walking along this street, he always felt he was touching the very soul of humanity. Here, he knew, people struggled to survive each day so they could square off against the next one. They asked for little more than the right to dream about a better future, a future they knew deep in their hearts would never come.

Finn didn't venture into this part of Los Angeles often, but when he did he was never sorry. He came when he was mentally and physically tired, when he'd pushed himself to the limit or even beyond, when he needed to walk away from the pressures of his life and touch base with something he couldn't clearly define.

He took a deep breath and laughed softly, realizing people would think he was insane for savoring the aromas of cabbage, exhaust fumes, rotting garbage, and sweat. It had been many months since he'd traveled to this world, and it felt good to be there. He *needed* to be there.

As he continued to walk, his artist's eyes missed no detail of his surroundings. But he would never put any of what he saw on canvas. He'd long ago decided he would never take any of this away to be used for his own gain. It gave him so much already, and he didn't return its gifts in kind.

Yes, he thought, he was probably nuts, an eccentric artist or some such thing. What he was, actually, was an *exhausted* artist. He had been laboring for months to prepare for his most recent private showing in an exclusive gallery on Rodeo Drive. Held two nights ago, it had been a huge success, his works selling for thousands of dollars a canvas. The critics were once again singing the praises of brilliant, talented, thirty-year-old Finn O'Casey.

Finn was grateful, humble, and tired.

He turned a corner and quickened his step as he headed for his favorite spot in the neighborhood, The Book Mark. The dusty, dirty used book store was a treasure chest of every kind of book imaginable. The owner, Bev Shaw, was a flamboyant woman, who dressed like a gypsy, laughed like an angel, and invited all and everyone to enter her chaotic establishment and browse to his heart's content.

Finn had been coming to this area of Los Angeles for nearly five years, and Bev never seemed to change. No matter how many months passed between his visits, she always greeted him with a hug and an offer of a cup of herbal tea.

Bev swore like a trooper, declared that those who abused power, money, and authority should take a flying leap, and had cried with joy when Finn had brought her a kitten three years ago. She'd immediately named it Keats, quoted "A thing of beauty is a joy forever" to it, and given Finn a loud, smacking kiss on the lips.

Finn smiled as he glanced up at the sign above the store. It was badly in need of a fresh coat of paint. With a tremendous feeling of anticipation, he entered The Book Mark.

Liberty stood at the far end of one of the narrow rows of high shelves, dusting books. Her head snapped up the moment she heard the tarnished bell over the front door jingle, announcing someone's entrance.

Part of her immediate attention was due to her desire to greet and offer assistance to customers. But she was also nervous, thanks to a restless night and vivid nightmares of a short, stocky man chasing her down rows and rows of crowded bookshelves.

She'd finally had enough, and escaped from her bed at dawn. After a light breakfast, she'd come down to the store to begin the tedious task of cleaning. Half an hour ago, at nine, she'd unlocked the front door and flipped the sigh to "open." There had been several customers since, none of whom remotely resembling the man in the shadows.

Liberty walked forward to greet this new customer, then stopped, surprised by the sudden rapid tempo of her heart.

Good heavens, she thought, what a beautiful—
yes, that was the appropriate word—a beautiful
man. He was standing just inside the door with
the morning sun pouring over him, turning his
blond hair nearly white, and his tanned skin a
warm, burnished bronze.

He was tall, over six feet, had wide shoulders, a
broad chest, and strong arms, all of which were
displayed marvelously by his yellow knit shirt. His
narrow hips and long, long legs were clad in faded
jeans that seemed to hug his body lovingly.

And that face. Lord above, he was handsome.
He had brown eyes, a straight nose, high cheek-
bones, a strong jaw and chin, and the most sensual, kissable lips she'd ever seen. Yes, he was
beautiful. No, maybe she'd trade in that word for
another. It alone wasn't enough to describe the
rugged appeal of this man. Raw masculinity and
blatant sensuality radiated from him.

Why, Liberty mused dryly, couldn't a virile spec-
imen like *that* decide to watch her from the shadows at night? After all, if she was going to be
scared out of her wits, she might as well go for
the gusto. *Oh, Liberty, shut up,* she lectured herself. That was the most absurd thought she'd had
in her entire life. *She* was the one spying from
the shadows at the moment.

She walked out of the row of shelves and smiled.
"Hello. May I help you?"

Finn turned his head at the sound of the lovely
voice, and his eyes widened slightly. The beauty
walking toward him definitely was not Bev Shaw.
Bev was not in her mid-twenties, didn't have wavy,

dark auburn hair tumbling to her shoulders, a very pretty face, and the biggest brown eyes he'd ever seen.

Bev also wasn't about five feet six, and never could have done that kind of justice to a pale green T-shirt and snug jeans. Nor did Bev have shapely legs that seemed to go on forever. Nope, that wasn't Bev Shaw. But whoever she was, she was certainly attractive, and the sudden flash of heat through his body said his libido knew it too.

"Hello?" Liberty said again, cocking her head.

Finn cleared his throat. "Yes, hello. You took me by surprise. My name is Finn O'Casey, and I dropped in to see Bev. I take it she isn't here?"

Liberty sighed and walked behind the counter. An ancient cash register sat on one end, and she had polished the scarred wood of the countertop to a dull shine, which was the best it was going to produce.

"No, she isn't here," she said, looking directly at Finn. "My aunt passed away over two weeks ago."

Finn frowned and strode over to the counter. "Bev . . . died?" He shook his head. "I can't believe it. She wasn't that old, and she always seemed to be bursting with energy. What happened?"

"I'm afraid I don't have many details, Mr. O'Casey. Apparently, she had a heart condition that took her very suddenly."

"Finn. Call me Finn. You're Bev's niece?"

"Yes, Liberty Shaw."

"She never mentioned any family."

"We weren't close. I only met Aunt Beverly once when I was a child. I was shocked when she left me this store in her will. I flew out from Chicago a couple of days ago." She glanced around. "I'm really not sure what I'm going to do with this place. I'm in the process of trying to clean it up at least. I'm sorry to have to inform you of my aunt's death, Mr . . . Finn. I've already come to realize that she had a great many friends, all of whom have been saddened by her death. I wish I'd had an opportunity to know her better. From what everyone who has come in here the last few days has said, Aunt Beverly was a remarkable woman."

Finn nodded. "She was. Bev was unique, very unusual. She took life as it came, always smiling. She followed her own set of rules, the world be hanged. She was totally refreshing, and collected people who cared about her like others collect stamps." He ran his hand over the back of his neck. "Damn. I wish I'd known. I could have at least gone to her funeral." He paused. "No, Bev wouldn't have liked that. She thought funerals were a waste of time."

"I know," Liberty said. "She left specific instructions about that with her attorney. He notified my father, who then had my mother write me. I still feel Aunt Beverly's family should have been here, but it wasn't what she wanted. Her attorney handled everything, then notified me that I'd inherited The Book Mark."

Finn smiled slightly. "Leave it to Bev to do things her way. Well, I'll miss her, and so will a lot of others, I'm sure. You said you weren't positive about what you're going to do with the store?"

"I'll try to sell it . . . I guess." Liberty laughed. "Yes, I'll sell it. You caught me with a case of teacher burnout at the end of an awful school year. Even this dusty place holds greater appeal than a classroom at the moment, but I have a signed contract to teach again next year in Chicago."

Finn gazed at her for a long moment, then a wide smile broke across his face. "Your laugh . . . it's exactly like Bev's. I loved the way she laughed. It was rich, sort of husky, and filled a room to overflowing."

"Wind chimes," Liberty said softly, meeting his gaze. "I can remember thinking that Aunt Beverly's laughter sounded like wind chimes. You've just paid me a lovely compliment, Finn, by saying my laughter is like hers. Thank you."

Neither moved as they continued to look at each other, both of them immobile under the other's scrutiny. A flutter danced along Liberty's spine, then tingled across her breasts. Heat coiled low in Finn's body. He felt his manhood stir, and was the first to break the eerie spell that had woven around them.

"Liberty," he said, hearing the grittiness in his voice. "That's an unusual name. I like it." Lord, he thought, his body was going crazy. He felt as though he'd been punched in the gut. Liberty Shaw was one very potent lady. "Liberty Shaw. Yes, I really like that. I assume since you're a Shaw that you're not married?" What in the hell difference did it make if she was married? He'd come there to see Bev. Bev was gone, so he'd be on his way. He'd never see Liberty Shaw again.

"No, I'm not married," she said. Liberty, don't ask him if *he's* married, she told herself firmly. He'd be leaving any minute now, and she'd never see him again. But when he'd looked at her for so long, she'd nearly fallen into a heap at his feet. She never reacted to a handsome man this way, yet she was definitely reacting to Finn O'Casey. Well, she certainly wasn't going to go any further with this nonsense and ask him if he was married. "Are *you* married?" she heard herself say. Oh, good grief.

"Me? No. No way." Finn shook his head. "My sister, Tabor, married a great guy named Jared Loring last summer. Now she thinks everyone should be marching down the aisle toward wedded bliss. She and Jared are terrific together, and I'm delighted that Tabor is so happy, but she's turning into a matchmaking menace." He laughed. "I wouldn't wish me on anyone."

Liberty smiled. "Why? Are you awful? A really rotten person?"

"I'm a painter. When I'm painting I lose all track of time. I wouldn't be too popular with a wife who expected me promptly at the table every night for dinner."

"If she loved you she'd understand," Liberty said. Well, listen to her. Since when was she an expert on love? "Oh, forget that. Maybe she wouldn't understand, I don't know. I've never been in love."

"Why not?"

She shrugged. "It just hasn't happened."

"You don't seem too worried about it."

"My friends tell me my biological clock will ring when I'm thirty and I'll go into a state of panic. I'm only twenty-six, so . . . You know, Finn, you're the only person who's come in here whom I've told

I didn't really know Aunt Beverly. It doesn't make sense to me why she left me this store, and I can't fathom why I've been trying to justify it to strangers. It's very easy to talk to you, I guess." It would also, she thought, be very easy to scramble across that counter and kiss those luscious lips of his. Oh, for Pete's sake, the dust must be addling her brain. "Well, I'd better get back to my scrubbing and rubbing. This place is a disaster."

"Are you living upstairs?"

"Yes."

He frowned. "This isn't a top-of-the-line neighborhood, Liberty. You're going to have to be very careful. Make sure your doors are locked, don't go out alone at night, that type of thing." Where was all this Boy Scout advice coming from? he wondered. Still, Liberty could find herself in real trouble down here.

"I intend to be very cautious. I've already been rather unsettled by . . ." Her voice trailed off.

Finn leaned toward her. "By?"

She waved one hand in a dismissive gesture. "Nothing. My imagination was working overtime."

"Humor me. What jangled you?"

"Really, Finn, I'm sure the man lives in the neighborhood and has been following the same pattern for years."

Finn stiffened. "What man? What pattern?"

"Well, he . . ." Liberty rolled her eyes. "This is going to sound so silly. Okay, for the two nights I've been here a man has been standing in the shadows across the street. From the way he tilts his head back, it appears to me that he's watching the windows of the apartment. He's probably out for his usual stroll, and stops to look at the stars, or whatever. I told you it was dumb. Forget I even mentioned it."

Finn's frown deepened. "It's not dumb at all. What does he look like?"

"Short and stocky, wearing dark clothes. I haven't been able to see his face clearly. I'm sure it's all very innocent."

"It probably is, but promise me you'll be careful."

"Yes. Yes, I will," she said softly.

Again, that strange spell wove itself around them as their gazes held for a long moment. And again, it was Finn who broke the silence.

"Where's Keats?" he asked, ignoring the heat pulsing low in his body.

Liberty blinked, bringing herself back from the hazy, sensual place she'd floated to. "You want a book of poems by Keats?"

"No, Keats is a big orange cat. I gave him to Bev three years ago when he was a kitten."

"I haven't seen a cat."

"He'll show up. He's probably mooching off someone in the neighborhood. Whoever is feeding him will stop once they know you're here, and Keats will get hungry and come home."

"Hungry," Liberty repeated. "You know, there's no cat food in the apartment, nothing to give a clue that Aunt Beverly had a pet."

"That's weird. She spoiled Keats rotten. I can't imagine her running out of food for him."

"There wasn't much food of any kind. The refrigerator was empty. There were a few canned goods in the cupboard, but that's all. Now that I think about it, it's as though Aunt Beverly had been prepared to leave. Oh, that's crazy. I know nothing about her personal habits. Maybe she hated to shop and picked up things as she needed them."

"Maybe for herself, but not Keats. She asked me to watch the store for her once so she could go to the store for cat food. She came back with a bag full of cans. She laughed and said Keats ate like a king, and she always made sure she had plenty on hand for him. Are you positive there weren't any cans of cat food in the cupboards?"

"Yes, I'm certain."

"Strange. Even if Bev hadn't been feeling well, she would have asked someone to shop for food for Keats."

"The lawyer assured me that no one had been in here. He gave me the keys. That eliminates the possibility of someone remembering Keats, and coming to get him and his food."

"Where was Bev when she died, Liberty?"

"She collapsed on the street. There was a card in her purse saying to contact the attorney in case of an emergency. One of the things he was to do was post a notice on the door of the store stating that Beverly Shaw has passed away."

"Well," Finn said, "I'm probably a product of watching too many detective movies, but this just doesn't add up. There's no way Bev would not have had food for Keats."

Liberty walked around the counter. "I'll prop the door open on the chance that Keats will wander in. This seems like a riddle, Finn, but I'm sure there's a reasonable explanation, just as there is for the man in the shadows."

"I guess you're right," he said.

He watched as Liberty moved past him, missing no detail of her very appealing figure, and catching a whiff of a light, floral cologne.

Liberty Shaw was simply beautiful, and he really didn't like the idea of her staying in the upstairs apartment alone. More, he didn't like the idea that he didn't like the idea. Great. He was mentally babbling.

But, dammit, she shouldn't be there alone. What if the joker she'd seen at night wasn't just out for a walk? And where in the hell was Keats? And why wasn't there any cat food in the cupboards? That was good. He'd go to the cops and report missing cat food, then watch himself get shipped to the funny farm.

Just after Liberty propped open the door, a young couple carrying a baby entered. Finn walked slowly through the store while Liberty helped the couple find a book on parenting.

Nearly half of the books and shelves, he noted, were already dust free. Liberty had worked hard since she'd arrived.

He picked up the dust cloth she had set on the shelf, took out the next book, cleaned it off, then put it back.

Chicago, he thought. That was where Liberty lived, and taught school, and would be returning to. By summer's end, and maybe sooner if she sold the store. She would disappear into the clouds, and he'd never see her again.

Why, he wondered as he continued to dust the books, was he not liking the thought of a quick "hello" and "good-bye" with Liberty Shaw? When he looked into her big, brown eyes, why did he feel trapped, like a butterfly snared in a net? And why in the hell did he have a driving, burning urge to haul Liberty into his arms and kiss her until neither of them could breathe? What was this auburn-haired beauty doing to him?

Finn's painting was, and always would be, his first love. There was no room in his life for a serious relationship, and the women he dated understood that. He kept no set schedule when he worked. He ate and slept when the mood struck, ignored clocks and the telephone, and certainly had no time to devote to being someone's "significant other."

Yes, he was a bit lonely at times, he admitted, yanking a book off the shelf. That was the price he paid for devoting himself to his art, for nurturing his talent instead of a budding romance. His hopes and dreams of making a name for himself in the art world were coming true at long last.

He did *not*, Finn told himself firmly, have protective instincts toward women—except for his sister—and especially not for one he'd just met. He did *not* fantasize about what it would be like to make sweet, slow love to said woman. He did *not* care if that woman left L.A. today, tomorrow, or whenever.

At the front of the store, Liberty laughed.

Dammit, Finn thought, shoving the book back onto the shelf, yes, he did care. Liberty Shaw was casting a spell over him, and he wasn't going to allow it to happen. His life was set up exactly the way he wanted it. He might suffer a little loneliness, but his life was perfect. As soon as Liberty was finished waiting on the young couple, he was going to tell her it had been nice meeting her, then hightail it out of there. And that would be that.

"Finn? Goodness, what are you doing?"

He jerked in surprise as Liberty's voice jarred him from his rambling thoughts. He turned to look at her. "Oh, I was just dusting the books, keeping busy." There should be a law against eyes that big, and brown, and warm. What would Liberty's eyes look like when she was consumed by desire . . . for him? When he moved over her and— O'Casey, can it! "You've . . . um, gotten a lot done already."

"Cleaning is the easy part," she said, walking slowly toward him. "There are boxes and boxes of books here in the store and upstairs in the apartment that should be sorted through. Plus, I found a box of correspondence of Aunt Beverly's. I flipped through a few of the envelopes, and they weren't even opened. She obviously wasn't what you would call an organized businesswoman, I'm afraid."

"She sure enjoyed life though," Finn said, smiling as Liberty stopped in front of him.

She really wished he wouldn't smile like that, Liberty thought. His smile was lethal. It lit up his handsome face like sunshine on a cloudy day, and caused her heart to skip a beat or two. And, darn it, she kept wondering what it would be like to be kissed by Finn O'Casey. Every time she looked at those lips of his, her mind went tripping off down a wanton road of wondering. Terrific, now she was getting poetic in her insanity.

"I must dust," she said.

"That rhymes," Finn said, chuckling. "Are you a poet?"

Lord, her brain really was deteriorating. "Nope," she said breezily, "not me." Luscious lips, beautiful body, magnificent man. Rhymes. "I don't have time to think up a rhyme." She burst into laughter. "Good grief, I did it again." She reached for the dust cloth he had placed on the shelf.

He trapped her hand with his. "I'll use this one if you have another."

Her smile faded. Such a strong hand, she thought, and so very warm. "Why?"

He shrugged. "Why not? I promised myself some time off after knocking myself out for the past few months. I don't have any pressing plans, so I'll dust books." What happened to his polite adieu and exit stage left? he asked himself. "Okay?"

"Well, I'd be foolish to turn down an offer of help, but this project isn't exactly a thrill a minute." The heat from Finn's hand had traveled up her arm, across her breasts, and had now landed in the pit of her stomach with a thud. Exciting, but almost frightening, heat. "I'll get another dust cloth." She attempted to pull her hand free, only to have Finn tighten his hold. "Finn?"

"When you were in high school," he said, "did you ever sneak a kiss in the stacks in the library?"

"No."

"Neither did I." He lifted his hand and slipped it beneath her hair at the nape of her neck. "I don't think people should go through life having missed that experience."

"Oh, well, I . . ." Praise be, she thought, he was going to kiss her. ". . . really don't want . . ." She sighed in defeat. "Yes, I do."

"Good." He lowered his head toward hers. "Then we're in complete agreement."

You'd better believe it, O'Casey, she thought dreamily.

Then Finn's lips claimed hers. . . .

Two

Finn's lips were commanding, yet gentle, and the heat within Liberty burst into raging fire, igniting her passion and heightening her senses. As his arms dropped to her back to bring her closer to his body, she wound her arms around his neck, parting her lips, glorying in the sensual invasion of his tongue.

Never, she thought, had she been kissed like this. Never had she responded with such overwhelming abandon. Never had she felt such burning need. There was strength in Finn's body, but he tempered it with tenderness, making her feel feminine and fragile and special. And oh, Lord, the heat!

She sank her fingers into his thick blond hair, urging his mouth harder onto hers. Her breasts were crushed against his muscled chest, and she savored the sweet pain, along with the feel of his lips and tongue mastering hers. A soft purr of pleasure hummed in her throat.

Finn was shocked and surprised that he was kissing Liberty Shaw. Just a minute ago he hadn't had the slightest intention of kissing her—but was he ever kissing her. His entire being seemed to be exploding from the sensual impact of her mouth moving beneath his, and her slender form nestled to his body.

Heat thrummed and coiled low in his body, and his manhood surged with aching need. He wanted Liberty Shaw with an intensity he'd never known before. It was like a flash fire overpowering him and his ability to reason. He drank of her sweetness as if he were a thirsty man trying to quell the burning within him, only to find that the taste of her fanned the flames even more.

It was only a kiss, his mind insisted.

Like no other kiss, a little voice within him whispered.

He'd just met this woman, said his mind.

He'd known her a lifetime, answered the whisper . . . but only now had she a name and form.

He had to stop kissing her, his mind demanded.

Later, came the whisper, later.

Now! his mind said.

Go to hell, the whisper said.

A groan rumbled up from Finn's chest, blocking out the sound of the battling voices in his head. His hands slid down over the gentle slope of Liberty's buttocks, and he spread his legs slightly to mold her to the cradle of his hips, his arousal hard and heavy against her.

He was slipping to the edge, he thought hazily.

He was losing control. That didn't happen to Finn O'Casey! He commanded his body and mind, as well as his emotions, holding a tight rein on each. Discipline had enabled him to stay on a straight road toward his goal of becoming an accomplished artist. He'd never allowed himself to be swayed by the lure of one woman, nor snared in the silken web of invisible threads that women had been known to weave around men's hearts. No, that didn't happen to Finn O'Casey, and it wasn't going to happen now, not for a heartbeat longer.

He tore his mouth from Liberty's and drew air into his lungs. He moved his hands to her shoulders and inched her away from his aching body.

She slowly lifted her lashes, and he groaned when he saw the dark desire in her big eyes. Her lips were moist and slightly parted in silent invitation for his mouth to take possession once more. With his last ounce of willpower, he took a step backward, dropping his hands to his sides. She staggered unsteadily for a moment, then blinked.

"Oh," she said breathlessly. "Oh, I . . . Oh, my."

"No joke," Finn said gruffly. He dragged one hand through his hair to keep from reaching for her again. A deep frown knitted his brows.

"That was—"

"A mistake," he said.

She took a deep breath and let it out slowly. "A mistake?" she repeated, then smiled. "Personally, I thought it was fantastic. You're definitely out of my league, Finn O'Casey, but I wouldn't have missed that kiss for the world. You've certainly had a lot of experience, haven't you? I have never in my life . . . Well, if you still want to help dust books I'd better go get another cloth." She turned and started away.

"Hey," he said. He strode after her, grabbed her arm, and spun her around to face him. "Wait just a damn minute here."

"Yes?" she asked pleasantly.

"What do you mean I'm out of your league?" he said loudly. "And what's this bull about my having a lot of experience? There's no call for insults here, Liberty Shaw."

"I didn't intend to insult you, I was merely stating facts. You've obviously kissed a great many women, and I must say, you certainly do it with expertise."

"Would you knock it off?" he yelled. "You make me sound like a sleazy hustler. That kiss was ours, yours and mine. I couldn't have kissed you like that, if you hadn't been kissing me like that back. Got it?" He closed his eyes and shook his head. "Why am I screaming in your face?" He opened his eyes and glared at her. "Liberty Shaw, you're driving me crazy."

"Finn O'Casey," she said, smiling at him warmly, "if you're going to give me half of the credit for that kiss, I gladly accept. It was wonderful." Her smile faded. "However, it isn't going to happen again. Definitely not." She pulled her arm free and turned once more.

His hand snapped right back to her arm, halting her step. "Hold it."

"Now what?" she asked, looking up at him.

"Why isn't it going to happen again?" He managed to keep his volume at a normal level.

"I'm not a naive child, Finn. I know danger

signals when I see . . . Well, feel them. I have never in my life experienced such instant . . . That is to say, if a kiss in the middle of a dusty bookstore can do what yours did to me, heaven forbid what might happen in a more romantic setting. I don't usually stand around discussing kisses, but that was no ordinary kiss either. Maybe you can handle this, but I can't. May I have my arm back, please?"

"What? Oh, yeah, sure." He dropped his hand to his side. "Go get another dust cloth."

She nodded and walked away.

Finn watched her go, watched the gentle swaying of her hips. Her buttocks had felt like heaven beneath his hands as he'd nestled her to his throbbing body. Realizing he was staring at her, he shook his head.

He was tired, he told himself, totally wiped out, both mentally and physically. Exhausted people were susceptible to things, like catching a cold, or the flu, or the bubonic plague. The fact that he wasn't handling, as Liberty so astutely put it, the impact of that kiss was due to his temporarily weakened condition. His feelings of protectiveness toward her also had to stem from his depleted energies. Liberty Shaw's overwhelming effect on his mind and body was because his mind and body were momentarily under par. There. Praise the Lord he'd figured *that* out. Everything was once more under control.

Liberty rummaged in a box behind the counter and found a fairly good sized and clean dust cloth.

She stood, then plunked her elbows on the counter-top and rested her chin in one hand as she stared into space.

She supposed she should be totally ashamed of herself for kissing Finn O'Casey the way she had. She certainly didn't go through life leaping into the arms of men she'd just met. And she'd never, ever, responded to a kiss the way she had to Finn's. She could still feel the heat pulsing deep within her, still taste the sweet flavor of his luscious lips on hers.

So? she asked herself. Why wasn't she mortified by her behavior? Why wasn't her conscience poking her in the code-of-conduct portion of her mind? Because she'd meant what she'd said. She wouldn't have missed that kiss for the world. She'd felt so gloriously alive, so feminine and beautiful. It was now a precious memory she could cherish, but it certainly could not, would not, happen again.

She straightened and shook her head. No, she reaffirmed to herself, there would be no more kisses shared with Finn. Something strange, exciting, and frightening had happened to her the moment she'd seen him standing in that waterfall of sunlight when he'd entered the store. She was going to take her one stolen kiss and tuck it away in a private chamber of her heart, and that would be that. Whether Finn was insulted by the statement or not, she knew he was most definitely out of her league.

With a decisive nod of her head, she marched back down the row of books. "Clean cloth," she said, shoving it at Finn. "You can finish this side." She wiggled past him, making sure she didn't touch him. "I'll start on this next bunch. Feel free to quit when you've had enough. This certainly isn't your problem."

Finn glanced at her as she began to dust. So damn beautiful, he mused. He snapped his head back around and yanked a book off a shelf.

They worked in silence for several minutes, then Liberty sneezed.

"Bless you," Finn said.

"Thank you. The dust is tickling my nose. I must say this is the most unique summer situation I've found myself in. Summer is my time for change, my do-something-different time each year before I start teaching again in the fall."

"What do you teach?"

"English Literature to high school students. I love books, always have." She laughed softly. "I now realize I like clean, dust-free books. Well, this place will be spruced up soon. I try to make it a practice not to find fault with my do-something-different time in the summer."

"Do you like teaching?"

She shrugged. "It's okay, but rather frustrating. My class is required for graduation, and the majority of the students aren't that interested in what I'm trying to teach them. Oh, there are a few who brighten my day, but not very many." She replaced a book and took out another. "By the end of the school year I need a change, and the summers save my sanity."

"Do you enjoy living in Chicago?"

"I have marvelous friends there."

"That's not the question. You never lose track

of real friends, no matter where you go. What about Chicago, the city?"

"I hate it," she said breezily. "Goodness, this book is old. I wonder if it's valuable simply because it's ancient."

"You hate living in Chicago?" He turned to look at her, leaning his forearm on the shelf.

She met his gaze across the several feet that separated them. "Yes. The winters are grim, and seem endless. The summers are hot and humid. Spring and autumn aren't so bad, but if you blink you miss them. I took the teaching position there when I graduated from college, and in all these years I haven't grown to like Chicago one bit."

"Then why do you stay?"

"Because I can."

He shook his head. "You've lost me."

"My father is career army, and we moved constantly all of my life. Some kids do fine with that life-style, but I never did. I'm an only child, and I was lonely. I dreaded starting in yet another new school when we moved. I loved being in college because I knew that for four years I didn't have to budge. When I was offered the job in Chicago, I made up my mind I was staying, no matter what. I finally had a choice, a voice, a sense of control over my life. My do-something-different summers balance things out a little. I was supposed to deliver telephone books this summer, but I'm here instead."

"You stay in a city you hate," he said slowly, "because you can."

"Precisely."

"I see." But he didn't, not really. Liberty was

intelligent and beautiful, and had professional skills that were in demand everywhere in the country. He could understand her need for stability and security after a childhood she'd never really adjusted to, but to stay in a place she detested was carrying the need too far. She'd said she'd never been in love, so there was no man keeping her in Chicago. She lived there because she could. Someone needed to get it across to Miss Liberty Shaw that being in control of one's life included the right to make choices and changes for the better. She'd been a victim of her father's career, but now she was a victim of herself.

"Hello?" a woman called. "Is anyone here?"

"Yes, I'm coming," Liberty answered. She slid past Finn and hurried to the front of the store.

Liberty's eyes widened when she saw the woman who was waiting by the counter. She was tall, appeared to be in her late thirties, and was dressed in a raw silk, turquoise-colored suit. Although she could shed fifteen pounds without missing them, her short blond hair was perfectly coiffured, her makeup applied with a practiced hand, and several large rings, adorning fingers with beautifully manicured nails, sparkled in the late morning sun.

The woman wasn't particularly pretty, Liberty thought. Her nose was large, her eyes heavy-lidded, her mouth too big for her face. But there was that intangible aura of wealth hovering over her. An invisible circle was drawn around her that said no one but the invited should venture too close. And to top it off, a white limousine was parked at the curb. Who was this woman, and what on earth was she doing in a dusty old bookstore in this part of town?

"May I help you?" Liberty asked, going behind the counter.

The woman's gaze swept quickly over Liberty, and she frowned.

"I must see Bev Shaw immediately," the woman said, a slight edge to her cultured voice. "I'm Victoria Manfield. Bev is expecting me. I wired her from London and said I was on my way."

"I'm sorry, Miss . . . Mrs. . . . ."

"Miss Manfield. Where is Bev? I don't have time to waste."

"My aunt Beverly passed away two weeks ago, Miss Manfield," Liberty said softly.

Victoria Manfield opened her mouth, shut it, then opened it again. "That is not humorous, young woman," she said stiffly. "Tell Bev that I'm here. She has something that belongs to me, and I must have it. I don't have the patience for silly games."

"This is no game, I assure you," Liberty said. "It was a shock to me as well."

"Dear God," the woman whispered. "You're serious."

"Yes."

"You called her your aunt Beverly. You're really her niece?"

"Yes, I am. I'm Liberty Shaw."

"Miss Shaw, I must have my property returned to me immediately. Did you inherit this store and your aunt's belongings?"

"Well, yes, but—"

"Did you find a small package with my name on

it? I called Bev from London and she said she had it. That was just over two weeks ago. She assured me she'd wrap it in plain paper, put my name on it, and keep it safe until I could get here. I had important business to attend to and simply couldn't get away. I phoned several days ago but there was no answer, so I finally sent a wire. And now you're saying that Bev is . . ." She pressed trembling hands to her cheeks for a moment. "My package must be here somewhere." She glanced around. "This place is a mess. The few times I've been here it's always looked like this. I assume Bev's apartment upstairs is in no better shape."

"A mess?" Liberty said, all innocence as she looked around. "Well, I guess it is a tad cluttered. But to quote Titus Lucretius Carus, 'What is food to one, is to others bitter poison.' My aunt Beverly and her friends apparently adored The Book Mark as is."

"Yes, fine," Victoria said, waving a hand dismissingly. "I want my package, Miss Shaw. Now."

"And I'd gladly give it to you, but I haven't seen anything with your name on it. Not that I've looked, of course, since I arrived such a short time ago. If you'd like to leave your telephone number, I'd be happy to call you the minute I—"

"That won't do," Victoria said shrilly. "It must be safely back in my possession this very minute."

Finn appeared from the shadows. "Miss Shaw said she hasn't come across it yet." He moved to stand beside Liberty. "Manfield. Would that be the Manfields who own a hefty chunk of California?"

Victoria stiffened. "I don't know who you are,

but I'm getting your message. You want money, don't you, in exchange for the package?"

"Hey," Finn said, raising his hands, "I didn't say that. I was simply wondering if you're who I think you are."

"You know I am," Victoria said, her voice rising. "Bev would never have tried to sell my own property back to me. She wasn't that kind of a person. She understood that it was a mistake that the— that what is mine ended up here. Trying to extort money from me is going to bring you more trouble than you can handle. I trust I'm making myself clear?"

Finn's jaw tightened. "Look, lady, you're jumping to the wrong conclusions. Don't try throwing your big-bucks weight around in this section of town. You're not on your own turf down here."

"Finn, please," Liberty said, placing one hand on his arm. "Miss Manfield, I'll look for your package, all right? And I promise you that I'll call you the minute I find it. I'll return it to you just as Aunt Beverly said she would. Perhaps if you told me exactly what I'm looking for, it would—"

"No!" Victoria interrupted. "It's mine, it's very personal. It's a small . . . book. Bev said she'd wrap it in plain paper. That's all you need to know. It's about four by six inches in size. I'm sentimentally attached to it, you see, and I was devastated to learn that my housekeeper had brought it down here with other discarded books. It was all a mistake, a terrible mistake. I must have it safely back in my hands before . . . Well, before something happens to it. It's not worth anything, you understand, except to me." She forced a smile. "Surely you can sympathize with a woman's sentimental attachment to something that has no monetary value, Miss Shaw."

"Yes, of course," Liberty said. "I'll call you just as soon as I find the package."

"No, no, that won't do. I'm terribly busy. I'll contact you. I assume you're staying in Bev's apartment?"

"Yes."

"Good. Fine. I'll be in touch very soon, very soon."

Victoria Manfield hurried from the store and a uniformed driver ran around the gleaming limousine to open the door for her. The huge car sped away.

"Well," Liberty said, looking up at Finn, "wasn't she something? The idle rich certainly get hyper about things, don't they? Imagine being in such a dither about a book she's sentimentally attached to. Well, it's not my place to stand in judgment as to what's important to a person. I still have a baby doll I got on my fourth birthday." She shrugged. "Maybe Victoria Manfield's treasure is from her childhood too. You know, a book of nursery rhymes or something."

Finn narrowed his eyes. "I don't think so," he said slowly.

"Why not?"

"Just a feeling, something I sensed in the mighty Miss Manfield. I could be imagining it, of course, because I don't know her personality, but I got the feeling she was more than just distressed because she'd lost a keepsake. She seemed . . . frightened."

Liberty looked first at the open doorway Victoria Manfield had rushed through, then back at Finn. "Frightened? Oh, Finn, that's silly. If I lost my baby doll I'd be unhappy, but certainly not frightened. Victoria Manfield said the book had only sentimental value. She's probably just a very high-strung woman."

"Maybe," he said. "Maybe not. Why don't we quit dusting for now and look for her book? Her highness is obviously going to be bugging you to death on the phone until it's found."

"I get the definite impression you didn't like her."

"I didn't like her superior attitude. You know 'I have money and you don't, so I'm better than you.' The Manfield empire is huge. They have their fingers in a lot of pies. The whole shebang is run by her parents, her brother, and her, along with a tremendously large staff, of course. The Manfields are always in the paper—the society columns, what charity they've donated to, which business they've bought out. The Manfields are busy little bees."

"Why would Victoria Manfield come all the way down here to The Book Mark?"

Finn shrugged. "Who knows? Maybe she was passing through one day and spotted it. I can't find fault with that. I wandered in here five years ago, and have been coming back ever since. Your aunt had a special magnetism, Liberty. Victoria Manfield said she'd been here a few times, and I can understand that. I drove all the way in from Beverly Hills to visit Bev."

"Beverly Hills?" Liberty repeated. "You must be a very successful artist. That's wonderful, Finn. I always love to hear that someone's dream has come true. You must have worked very hard, but that doesn't always bring the rainbow. I'm so pleased for you."

"Thank you," he said, surprised at her words. "Usually when I say I live in Beverly Hills, someone makes a reference to my money. But you centered on my achieving my dream. That's nice, Liberty, really nice."

"Money isn't all that important if a person isn't happy," she said softly.

He drew his thumbs lightly over her cheeks. "You're right. There are a helluva lot of people who don't know that though. They think money is the end all and be all."

A shiver coursed through Liberty as Finn continued those tantalizing strokes across her cheeks.

An artist's hands, she mused, able to create works of beauty on canvas. Strong hands, tender hands, hands with such incredible heat radiating from them. How would those hands of the artist feel skimming over her bare body? What did Finn see with his discerning eyes when he looked at her? What image of her would he capture forever in oils if he painted her?

" 'The painter's brush consumes his dreams,' " she whispered, looking deeply into his eyes.

"William Butler Yeats," he said, his voice husky. He sighed and dropped his hands from her face. "It's true, that quote. The brushes, the oils, the picture that hasn't been painted yet, they all consume my dreams, my thoughts, even my very soul, not leaving room for anything else." He took a step backward and shook his head. "Listen to me.

I sound like I'm complaining, feeling sorry for myself. I'm not, Liberty. I've worked hard, I'm very grateful for my success and the support I had from my father and Tabor over the years. I'm making a name for myself in the art world, and that's what I've always wanted."

She looked at him for a long moment before she spoke. "I asked a writer to speak to my classes one day this year," she said quietly. "One of the things he told my students is that being a writer is a lonely business. He said he assumed that that held true for artists and composers, all those in the arts who have to work alone to create what is burning inside them. He said the writer must write, the painter must paint, and on and on, in order to be complete, to have happiness and inner peace. That's true, isn't it?"

Finn nodded. "Yes."

"And painting, like writing, is a lonely business." She paused. "Are you lonely, Finn?"

Dear God, he thought, panic rushing through him. He felt stripped bare, the very essence of himself exposed to Liberty Shaw. He'd never spoken like this to anyone. Not Tabor, his father, his agent, who was also his friend, no one. With her soft voice and big brown eyes filled with understanding, Liberty seemed to be touching his soul. She was forcing him to look deep within himself for answers to questions he'd only addressed for fleeting moments. He'd known for a long time that the life he'd chosen for himself included being lonely, but she was making him take stock of just how chilling that loneliness was. Dammit, he'd had enough of this.

"Finn?"

"Yes," he heard himself say. "Yes, I'm lonely." He reached out and pulled her to him, holding her tightly to him and burying his face in the fragrant cloud of her auburn hair. "Liberty Shaw," he murmured, "what are you doing to me?"

She wrapped her arms around his waist and rested her head on his chest. She could hear the steady beat of his heart, feel his heat and strength, and she gloried in all that was Finn.

"I'm sorry," she whispered. "I didn't mean to pry." And, she thought, she hadn't meant to care about this man with such a strange and frightening intensity. She didn't want Finn to be lonely. She'd known loneliness as she was growing up, and it was an evil companion that gained power in the darkness of night. Finn shouldn't be lonely. Not Finn.

He lifted his head and gently stroked the top of her head with his chin, not loosening his hold on her. "You caught me at a bad time, Liberty. I'm physically tired and mentally drained because I've been pushing for months to get ready for a showing of my work that just took place. That's why I came down here to see Bev. I come when I need to escape from it all, to put it away and give myself a chance to recharge. You're not seeing me at my best."

"But perhaps . . . Well, maybe I'm seeing you as you really are," she said, her head still nestled against his chest. "There's no shame in admitting that you're lonely, Finn. It doesn't rob you of anything, make you less of a man. I understand loneliness because I grew up with it. That's why I stay in Chicago. I'm surrounded by friends who care about me, and I'm not lonely there. I don't like the city, but I need what it offers me, and I finally have a choice in the matter. Maybe it's time for you to make a choice too. Maybe it's time for you to make room in your life for something, some-one, in addition to your art. Only you can answer that."

"There isn't room," he said. Was there? "No." But what had his agent said after the show? "You've made it to the big time, kid. Now you can start living a little, put some balance in your life, Finn." He'd heard the words, but was only now allowing them to sink in. Liberty was forcing him to take an inventory of his entire life, weigh and measure it. He'd just met this woman! Yet he felt as though he'd known her for a lifetime. Dammit, he was tired, that was all. He was blowing all of this out of proportion. "No, Liberty, my life is set up ex-actly how I want it. I just need some time off, then I'll be fine. I always am."

She lifted her head to look at him. "Like my do-something-different summers?"

He pulled his gaze from hers and stared at a spot on the wall. "Yeah," he said gruffly, "exactly."

"I see."

That, he thought, was what was shaking him to the core. She seemed able to see all the way to his soul. He didn't like this, not one damn bit. His feelings of loneliness would get pushed back into the shadows where they belonged as soon as he was rested.

"So!" he said, forcing a lightness to his voice. He slowly, reluctantly, set her away from him.

"While I'm in my do-something-different mode like you are, let's start searching for Money Manfield's package. Okay?" He shifted his gaze to her. She was looking intently at him. "Is my nose on upside down?"

"No," she said, managing a smile. Finn was running, she thought. Running from himself. But there was nowhere to hide from loneliness. He had to fight back, make choices and changes, but he wasn't ready to admit that. So be it. It wasn't like her to step into someone's private space as she'd done to Finn, but it made her heart ache to think of him being lonely. Yet this didn't make sense. She hardly knew Finn. "Okay. The package. Victoria Manfield said Aunt Beverly was going to put it in a safe place." She glanced around. "Nothing looks safe. It just looks messy."

Finn chuckled. "You're right. My guess is that it's in the apartment upstairs." He glanced at his watch. "It's lunchtime. Bev just locked up for an hour, and people know that. Why don't I go get some sandwiches, then after we eat we can look around the apartment for the package?"

Liberty shrugged. "Sounds fine to me. The sooner that package is returned to Victoria Manfield, the better. I have a feeling she's going to be calling regularly to see if I've found it."

"You're right. I'll go get us some lunch." He slid his hand to the nape of her neck, lowered his head, and kissed her very thoroughly. "I needed that." He turned and strode out of the store.

Liberty took a steadying breath, then pressed one fingertip to her lips. "Mercy," she said. Her heart was racing again. What Finn O'Casey could do to her with a kiss was sinful. And delicious. And exciting, and frightening, and . . . "Shut up, Liberty."

When Finn returned carrying a brown paper bag, Liberty locked the store and moved the plastic hands on the faded cardboard clock that hung on the door to indicate the time The Book Mark would open again.

"There," she said. "Follow me, sir, to the upper eaves, which are more cluttered than down here."

"There's no outside entrance to the apartment?" he asked.

"No, the stairs are in the back of the store. Ready?"

"After you, ma'am," he said, with a sweep of his arm.

He followed Liberty to the rear of the building, then up a narrow, dark staircase. He was under control . . . again, he thought dryly. He'd lectured himself while he'd trudged to the cafe and back, and was determined that there would be no more heavy-duty, soul-searching discussions with Miss Liberty Shaw. He was going to keep it light, enjoy her company and the atmosphere of the crummy, dusty, intriguing little bookstore.

And he was going to kiss her every chance he got.

Not wise? Too bad, he'd decided. Kissing Liberty was heaven itself. He knew this was temporary, was do-something-different time for both of them, so why not savor the ecstasy of more of those kisses? As for being lonely, he'd shoved that back into a corner of his mind where it belonged. And it was going to stay there. He was totally in command of himself again.

"Ta-da," Liberty said as they entered the apartment.

"Grim," he said. "Bev must have bought every book that was offered to her. She probably didn't have the heart to say no to anyone."

"Well, let's eat first," Liberty said.

"I bought drinks too," he said, sitting down at the table. "I hope you like what I got."

"I'm not fussy."

He unpacked the bag, and they took bites from thick turkey sandwiches.

"Delicious," Liberty said. "I don't think the boxes are the place to start looking for the package, Finn. Somewhere safe would be a drawer or a shelf. Of course, I don't know how Aunt Beverly's mind worked. It wasn't along the lines of organized, that's for sure."

"I assume all of her clothes, personal belongings, what have you, are still here?"

"Yes, but she didn't have many clothes, and half of the dresser was empty."

"Really? She obviously enjoyed outrageous outfits, so I thought she'd have a lot of clothes. She seemed to have a shawl in every color in the rainbow."

Liberty stiffened in her chair. "Finn, there were no shawls in the closet or dresser. Not one. Did Aunt Beverly still wear a lot of bracelets and beads?"

"Yes," he said, nodding. "Costume jewelry, gawdy, fun stuff."

"It's not here."

"Are you sure?"

"Yes, I'm positive. When I unpacked there was plenty of room for my things without disturbing hers because she simply didn't have much. I didn't dwell on it at the time, but where are her shawls and jewelry?" Her eyes widened. "Finn, something isn't right here."

"Take it easy, Liberty. Maybe Bev knew she was ill and gave her things to people she cared about. That would explain the absence of the cat food and Keats himself. She might have found a home for him where she knew he'd be loved."

"Well, maybe," Liberty said slowly.

"Except . . ."

"Except what?"

"I don't know," he said, running a hand over the back of his neck. "I suppose Bev could have been very organized about all that, but it doesn't fit how she handled things in general. And why not keep her possessions, especially Keats, with her and simply leave instructions with her lawyer as to who got what? I don't mean to sound cold, but she couldn't have known *exactly* when she was going to die. A doctor doesn't say to a patient that they're going to buy the farm next Tuesday, or whatever."

Liberty frowned. "I see what you mean. But then again, she might have wanted to give Keats, the shawls, the jewelry to people herself, like gifts." She shook her head. "No, now wait a minute. Some of the people who have come by since I've been here were very close to Aunt Beverly, had been friends of hers for years. Not one of them seemed to know she was ill, and there was no mention of receiving anything from her."

"Liberty, Bev wore a lot of makeup. Her eye shadow always matched her shawl. Have you looked in the medicine cabinet in the bathroom?"

"No, I haven't opened it yet. I have a small cosmetic case I put on the sink with my toothbrush." She got to her feet. "I'll go check."

A few minutes later, Liberty came back into the room and sank onto her chair with a thud.

"You're pale as a ghost," Finn said. "What's wrong?"

"The medicine cabinet is empty. Even her toothbrush and toothpaste are gone. The lawyer assured me that no one had been in here. Oh, Finn, this is frightening. There are just too many riddles, things that don't make sense."

"You're right," he said. "Bev was eccentric, but no one packs her toothbrush and makeup so she'll be ready to attend her own funeral!"

Three

Liberty started to speak, changed her mind, and took a bite of sandwich instead. She chewed, swallowed, and glared at Finn.

"This is absurd," she said finally. "Schoolteachers from Chicago don't suddenly find themselves involved in the middle of mysteries. In the movies, maybe, or in books, but not in real life, Mr. O'Casey. We're behaving like brainwashed products of our environment who watch too much television."

Finn shrugged. "You have to admit that the way this adds up, it doesn't add up."

"You," she said, laughing, "are no smooth talking Spenser." She frowned. "I wish you'd smile. You're making me nervous sitting there looking so serious." She took another bite of sandwich, and glared at him again for good measure.

"Let me give you a little of my background data," he said. "Tabor's and my mother died when we were very young and our father, who passed away last year, raised us. Our father was Cat O'Casey, one of the best government agents ever to come down the pike."

Liberty nearly choked on her sandwich, and quickly took a drink. "Agent? As in, spy?"

"Not exactly. He performed specialized assignments for the government. There's no harm in talking about it now that he's gone, but while Tabor and I were growing up, we knew it never went outside the house. It was a way of life to us, what our father did for a living. We accepted it as a matter of course, no big deal, and we loved him very much."

"Amazing. Go on."

"Cat vowed to never lie to his children, so he told us about his assignments, adding more of the details as we grew older."

"Details?" she squeaked. "Gory details?"

"Yep. Cat also trained us from a very early age in self-defense, how to shoot a gun, pick a lock, override security systems, all kinds of terrific stuff."

"Amazing," Liberty repeated, her eyes wide.

"Both Tabor and I inherited our mother's artistic talent. I went on to oil painting, Tabor to interior decorating. Cat said that was fine, that we should follow our own path. He'd shared with us what he knew, who he was, and we were grateful that he'd never shut us out of his life. Tabor and I became involved in finishing Cat's last assignment as a legacy to him because he died before it was completed. It went a bit haywire, and Tabor had to go to Jared Loring for help after I got myself kidnapped by Mickey the Mouse Mason."

"Oh-h-h," Liberty moaned, "tell me this is a joke. You're kidding, right?"

"Nope."

"I was afraid of that."

"Anyway, Jared took charge and it all ended up fine after a couple more snafus. Tabor and Jared fell in love, and they're married and living in Las Vegas. Jared owns half a casino called Miracles with another man, Tucker Boone. There are great people on the Miracles staff: Nick, Trig, Turtle, Pico . . . Oh, Nick married a great woman named Pippa shortly after Tabor and Jared were married. Tabor was in seventh heaven about that, and was more determined than ever to see me tie the knot. The point is, Liberty, because of my father, Jared, and some of the others, I'm not exactly a stranger to the darker side of life. I grew up trained to watch and listen, to pay attention. I've learned to just go about my business, but I'm telling you, the facts surrounding Bev Shaw don't add up."

Liberty leaned toward him. "Maybe they do. Maybe there are very simple explanations for everything, Finn, but it just seems fishy at the moment. Yes. Your father's job and what he taught you about it are causing you to jump to conclusions. How's that?"

"I don't think so."

"Oh, please, Finn, think so. You're scaring me to death. Erase that. I didn't say 'death.' "

He trapped one of her hands with his on top of the table. "Whoa. Calm down. Face it, Liberty, what we've found isn't the normal setup when someone dies unexpectedly. Where are Bev's things —her makeup, her toothbrush, her favorite shawls and jewelry? Where is Keats and the cat food? Why is it looking more and more like Bev packed up and left?"

Liberty yanked her hand free. "That's ridiculous. I've seen and spoken with her lawyer, remember? He took care of the funeral arrangements for Aunt Beverly, then executed her will and notified me that I'd inherited The Book Mark."

"Fine," Finn said, getting to his feet. "That's where we'll start."

"Start what?"

"Finding the answers to what are too many questions. Let's go."

Liberty stood up. "We're going to see the lawyer?"

"Yep."

"But what about the store? And we're supposed to be looking for Victoria Manfield's package."

"Victoria Manfield can just stew for a while. As for The Book Mark, change the hands on your cute little cardboard clock to say you'll be open again at nine tomorrow morning."

"All right, Travis McGee, we'll go see the lawyer. Boy, are you going to feel dumb when he gives you all the information about Aunt Beverly's funeral. This is probably very disrespectful to someone who has passed away, but I'll humor you. Besides . . ."

"Yes?" Finn asked, raising his eyebrows.

"Well, it would be awfully comforting to know where Aunt Beverly's personal things are, and to be told that Keats is safely with whomever."

Finn laughed. "Whomever?"

She sniffed indignantly. "I'm an English teacher.

I'm obligated to say 'whomever.' I owe it to my profession."

"Oh, I see." He tried not to smile, but failed miserably.

"Can it, Fletch. We've got a caper to case."

"Good Lord," he said, chuckling. "Have you read every hard-boiled detective novel ever written?"

"Chicago winters are very long. I read all kinds of things. Last winter I hit the detective section of the library. I'm not without knowledge in this endeavor, Peter Finley."

Finn dropped his face into his hands and shook his head. "Spare me."

"Have you no faith?"

"No!"

Beverly Shaw's attorney, Liberty informed Finn, had an office six blocks from The Book Mark. Since Finn's car was parked eight blocks away, the decision to walk to the lawyer's was no contest.

"His name is Clarence Smith," Liberty said as they strolled along the trash-littered sidewalk. "He's about sixty, I guess, short, round, looks remarkably like Santa Claus. A sweetie pie."

"Mmm."

"He was very sympathetic about Aunt Beverly's death. He said they had been friends for many years, and he wished me luck with The Book Mark."

"Mmm."

"Spenser doesn't mumble 'mmm.' He always has a snappy retort."

"Mmm."

"Forget it," Liberty said, throwing up her hands.

Finn smiled but kept silent. Liberty Shaw, he decided, was really something. She was also a contradiction within herself. She stayed in Chicago for the sense of stability it gave her, but had the ability, whether she realized it or not, to shift gears and go with the flow depending on the situation she found herself in. The women he knew would have taken one look at The Book Mark and the neighborhood, and hightailed it home. But not Liberty. Now, she was marching along the dirty sidewalk like half of the team of Hart and Hart. Yes, she was really something.

"This is the building," Liberty said finally.

Finn glanced up at the deteriorating structure. "High-rent district."

"It's not wonderful, but I can picture Aunt Beverly giving her business to a friend. Clarence Smith's office is on the fourth floor."

As Finn followed Liberty up the dark, creaking stairs, he glanced at the doors they passed on the first three floors.

"Did you notice that all of these offices are empty?" he asked.

"No, I wasn't paying any attention."

"Mmm."

On the fourth floor, Liberty pointed down a narrow corridor. "There at the end, that's his office."

"After you, Sam."

"Sam?"

"Spade."

"You're showing your age, O'Casey."

"I'm an old thirty, Shaw."

At the office door, Liberty stopped so abruptly, Finn bumped into her.

"What's wrong?" he asked.

"The sign is gone. There was a stenciled sign that said, Clarence Smith, Attorney-at-Law, on the door."

"Maybe someone, whomever, copped it for a souvenir. Go on in."

Liberty turned the knob and pushed the door open, the squeaking hinges seeming to scream in the suddenly too silent building. The next sound she heard was the wild beating of her heart echoing in her ears.

The office was totally empty.

"Oh, Lord," she whispered, walking slowly forward.

Finn followed her. "Clean as a whistle. Clarence Smith has flown the coop."

She spun around to face him. "Finn, I don't understand this. He was here, I swear it. He was sitting behind a desk. I sat in a chair, there was a gray dented filing cabinet against the wall."

"I believe you," Finn said. He wandered around the empty room, then returned to stand in front of her. "They set it up to look legit, even lugged the stuff to the fourth floor to make it seem more permanent. Smith did his business with you, end of show."

"*They* set it up? They who?"

"I think it's 'whom.' "

"Finn!"

He placed his hands on her shoulders, and his voice was gentle when he spoke. "Liberty, there is obviously something nutso going on here, but I can't believe for one minute that the Bev Shaw I knew—know—would put her niece in any kind of danger. The thing is, we can't be sure that Bev is behind this."

"What do you mean?"

"She could be a pawn in someone else's game."

"What game? And why involve me? Do you think Aunt Beverly is alive?"

He nodded. "Everything points to it. She, or someone else, wants to make it appear that she's dead, but I'm betting she isn't. I think she packed her belongings, including Keats and his food, and left. Whether or not it was by her own choice, I don't know. To carry out the charade to the maximum, you inherited The Book Mark."

"But why? Oh, damn, damn, damn, what is going on here? Finn, this is frightening."

"No, it's just confusing at this point."

"What do we do next?"

"Hey, come here," he said, pulling her close. "You're shaking like a leaf." He wrapped his arms around her and held her tightly. "You're not alone, you know. I'm right here with you."

And he felt so good, Liberty thought, nestling closer to his muscled body. Dear heaven, she was suddenly in the middle of a nightmare. But Finn was there. He was holding her in the safe circle of his arms. She'd just stay right there pressed against him, and forget the rest of the nonsense that was happening to her. Oh, yes, she did like being held in Finn O'Casey's arms.

She tipped her head back to look up at him, managing a weak smile. "I must say, this is not a run-of-the-mill do-something-different summer." Because Finn was there. No, no, she'd meant because of the mystery surrounding Aunt Beverly. But then again . . . Oh, Liberty, don't think. "I'm not going to fall apart, Finn."

"You're also," he said, his voice husky as he lowered his head toward hers, "not going to go through this alone."

"But it's not your problem."

"Isn't it?" he murmured, then his mouth melted over hers.

What happened to not kissing Finn O'Casey again? Liberty wondered. Forget it. Not kissing Finn had been a dumb idea in the first place, because kissing Finn was . . .

All thought fled Liberty's mind as Finn parted her lips, his tongue delving deep into the darkness of her mouth to meet her tongue. Her arms floated up to twine around his neck, her breasts were crushed against his chest, and she answered the demands of his lips and tongue in total abandon. The heat, the heat of Finn, swept through her body, igniting her passion like a burning torch on a consuming journey of fire. Liquid fire. Hot.

Dear Lord, Finn thought hazily, he wanted Liberty Shaw with a driving need like nothing he'd ever known. The mere touch of her lips sent sensations rocketing through him like molten lava rushing out of control. There was no way he could remain detached, could retain command of himself. To kiss, to hold, to touch Liberty, was to want to make love to her for hours, through the sultry darkness of night and on to the rosy, glowing hues of dawn's light. The urge to sheath his aching manhood in the silken warmth of her femininity, to become one with her, was overpowering.

And Finn knew, despite the passion-laden fog in his mind, that his desire for Liberty went further than the physical. Emotions were intertwined as well. The fervent need to protect her from harm, to comfort her and erase the fear he'd seen in her eyes was growing ever stronger. He wanted to stand between Liberty and anything that might cause her distress.

He was being pulled, both physically and emotionally, into a place where he had never been, nor was he sure he wanted to be. Liberty was spinning a web around his heart, mind, and body. A web he had always avoided for fear it would hold him fast. And this web was a more dangerous web than most, because Liberty had no idea that she was doing it. He could be snared forever, then helplessly watch her fly away when her do-something-different summer was over.

He drew in a rough breath, then took possession of her mouth again, unable to stop himself from drinking of her sweetness. His whole body ached with desire for her, the heat within him churning and twisting in painfully tightening coils.

He had to get away from this woman before it was too late!

Yet he knew he couldn't leave her alone to face the tower of unanswered questions about Bev.

He told himself he had to stay with Liberty for now, just for now, then he would return to the safe world of his art when the mystery of Bev Shaw was solved.

His safe, lonely world.

Dammit.

"Dammit," he said, tearing his mouth from Liberty's.

He pulled her arms from his neck and moved around her to walk to the grimy window. He braced his hands high on the wooden frame and stared out, willing his body back under his control.

Liberty floated slowly down from the sensuous, misty place she had been transported to by Finn's magical touch. She blinked several times, drew a shaky breath, then turned slowly to look at Finn. She could feel the tension emanating from his rigid body.

The silence hung heavily in the empty room.

" 'The web of our life is of a mingled yarn, good and ill together.' " Finn finally said in a low voice.

"Shakespeare," Liberty said absently. "Finn, are you angry?"

His hold on the window frame tightened for a moment, then he shook his head. He turned to face her, shoving his hands into his back pockets.

"Angry?" he repeated, his voice still rough. "Only at myself, Liberty. I took you into my arms to comfort you because you were frightened, and before I knew it I was . . . I don't seem to have any control with you. When I kiss you I don't want to stop. And I want more. I envision myself taking off your clothes . . . slowly, very slowly . . . and kissing every inch of your dewy skin."

"Finn . . ." Liberty started, feeling a warm flush on her cheeks. Heat was still throbbing deep and low within her.

"And," he went on, "I picture making love to you. Beautiful, exquisite love, for hours and hours." A muscle jerked in his jaw. "And as if that isn't enough to tie me in knots, I also want to protect you, keep you from harm, be certain that you're no longer frightened by anything or anyone." He pulled his hands free of his pockets, and dragged one through his hair. "I'm not behaving true to form around you, Miss Shaw," he said, his voice rising. "Not one damn bit. And I don't like it one damn bit either. Got that?"

"I—"

"*I* control my body and mind," he said, thumping himself on the chest. "I don't get snared in feminine webs, even if the web is being spun by someone who doesn't even know she's spinning it."

Liberty frowned. "Huh?"

"Oh, hell," he said, throwing up his hands, "this is crazy. You"—he pointed a finger at her—"are a menace."

Liberty planted her hands on her hips. "That, Mr. O'Casey, is the most insulting thing I have ever heard. A menace? Me? Why? Because I enjoy kissing you? Because I have never responded to a man's kisses the way I do to yours? Well, excuse me all the way to hell and back, but I don't seem to have much control in regard to you either. However, you don't see me getting all hyper and nasty about it, do you? No, you do not. I could accuse you of trying to seduce me, bub, but I have no intention of doing that because I know I could put a stop to those kisses if I wanted to. You're not the only one not behaving true to form. I'm not exactly in the habit of melting into the arms of a man I barely know. There's something about you that makes me forget how to think clearly once you touch me. I'm not the menace here, you are. So from here on out, O'Casey, keep your luscious lips to yourself." She folded her arms over her breasts and lifted her chin. "Got that?"

"I . . . Well . . ." Finn cleared his throat. "You certainly have a temper when you get rolling, don't you? Somewhere in there I think you told me what I could do with myself, as in taking a long walk off a short pier." He shook his head. "Bub? Who says that? Spenser or Fletch?"

"That caps it, O'Casey," Liberty said, narrowing her eyes. "Try on 'dead meat' for size . . . *bub*." She spun around and marched toward the door.

"Wait a minute."

"No!"

"Liberty, please," Finn said quietly. "Please don't go out that door."

That was *not* fair, Liberty fumed, stopping in her tracks. How dare he speak in that soft, gentle, sexy voice after yelling his head off? Not fair at all. Well, she certainly wasn't going to turn around and look at him.

She turned around and looked at him.

Finn walked slowly toward her.

There was, she thought frantically as she backed up, a strange glint in Finn's brown eyes, and that loose, gliding motion of his body reminded her of a jungle cat stalking its prey. Oh, mercy, she'd lost control of her temper, and now she was in a heap of trouble.

She thudded against the wall, wondering where the door had disappeared to, and watched wide-eyed as Finn closed the remaining distance between them. He flattened his hands on the wall on either side of her head and stared down into her eyes, keeping his body away from her.

"It would seem, Miss Shaw," he said softly, "that we have a mutually shared problem. What do you think we should do about it?"

"Well, my word, Finn, how on earth should I know? I've never experienced anything like this before." She paused. "Lust. Maybe it's pure and simple lust. Oh, Lord. That sounds awful."

"No, it's not lust," Finn said thoughtfully. "Lust, I'd recognize. I've been down that road."

"Well, whoop-de-do for you," she said, glaring up at him. "Did you have a nice trip?"

"Not really. Anyway, cancel lust."

"Fine," she said, rolling her eyes heavenward. "Would you please move your carcass? I feel like a trapped mouse. Move."

"No."

"Oh."

"We're communicating here, Liberty, on an adult level. That's very important. So, okay, we're on the same wavelength. Something is happening between us, to us, that is very new, strange, different from anything either of us has experienced before. Check?" He waited. "Liberty?"

"Oh, yes, check," she said, nodding. "Now will you move?"

"No."

"Wonderful," she muttered. He was so close, she could feel his heat, smell that male scent that was uniquely his. He had to move before she leaned forward and plastered herself against every delicious, rugged inch of him. Oh, Lord, if she did that she'd never speak to herself again.

"I think," Finn said, "that we should just go with the flow."

"I beg your pardon?"

"We can't ignore whatever this is, Liberty, and I, for one, don't like unsolved riddles. You, me, us together, is a riddle. We can't seem to fight it, so we'll join it. If we want to kiss each other, we will."

Fantastic idea, Liberty thought. "I'm not certain that's a good idea, Finn," she forced herself to say.

"Sure it is. It's the only way to figure out what's happening. Hey, for all we know, we're products of the do-something-different mode. We've stepped away from our work, our normal day-to-day routine, and therefore we're functioning in an abnormal way. That's just one theory, of course. We'll know soon enough if it's true. So, what do you say? Should we try it? Go with whatever feels right at the time?"

"Well, I don't think . . ."

He moved closer to her. "Don't you want to know what this is, Liberty?" Closer. "Don't you want to solve the riddle?" His body brushed against hers.

"Guess so," she whispered, hardly able to breathe.

"Good. See what communication can accomplish?"

"It's a real pip . . . communication. Where would the world be if people didn't communicate? And, Finn, you have one second to kiss me, or I'm going to crawl up your body."

"Check."

He wove his fingers through her silky hair at

the same moment his mouth came down hard on hers. He pressed his body firmly against her as his tongue sought entry to the sweet, dark haven of her mouth.

Liberty wrapped her arms around his waist and met his tongue with her own, savoring the taste and feel of him. She didn't think, refused to think. She simply gave way to the sensations swirling within her.

Later, her mind whispered, she'd think. Right now it was just . . . go with the flow.

He was certifiably insane, Finn thought as his tongue danced and dueled with Liberty's. But the image of her walking out that door in a huff had sent icy panic rushing through him.

He blithered on like an idiot to convince Liberty to stay. But why in the hell was he moving full-steam-ahead into a place that was virtually scream-ing with danger signals? Did he really want the answer to what was happening between them? Hell, he didn't know. He'd think about it later . . . later. . . .

The kiss intensified, growing hungry, urgent, frenzied. Passions flared to a fever pitch. Finn groaned deep in his chest. A soft purr caught in Liberty's throat. And the kiss went on and on.

The intrusive noise came from a faraway place, inching into Finn's mind, forcing him back to reality. He stiffened as he raised his head and drew in a rough breath.

"Liberty," he said in a raspy voice, "there's some-one coming up the stairs."

"What?" she asked, slowly opening her eyes.

"Shh. Listen."

She nodded. "Yes," she whispered, "I hear footsteps. Oh, good grief, who do you think it is?"

"There's only one way to find out," he said, reaching for the doorknob.

"Finn, no, what if it's a burglar?"

"There's nothing in this building to burgle. It's probably just a wino looking for a place to crash. Shh."

He opened the door and peered out. Liberty moved behind him, bent down, and looked out beneath his arm.

A man had just left the stairs and was starting down the corridor toward them. He was short and round, and dressed in baggy pants and a faded shirt.

"Oh," Liberty whispered, "that's Clarence Smith. That's him, Finn, the lawyer I met with in this office."

"Shh!"

The man stopped, squinted, then quickly turned and headed back toward the stairs.

"Damn," Finn said, flinging open the door. "Hold it, Smith!" he yelled. "I want to talk to you."

Clarence Smith took off at a run, thundering down the stairs. Finn barreled out the door with Liberty right behind him.

"Stay here," he called over his shoulder.

"Not on your life, bub."

"Dammit," Finn muttered, then started down the stairs at full speed.

Liberty scrambled after Finn, but was unable to keep up with his long-legged stride. He disappeared from view as she hurried down the dark staircase. Suddenly she heard a loud crash and a muffled "oomph."

"Oh, my God," she whispered, and raced down the stairs.

On the second floor she saw Finn spread-eagle on his back, a large, dented wastebasket rocking back and forth near his feet.

"Oh, Finn. Oh, Finn. Oh, Finn." She dropped to her knees beside him. "Open your eyes, please, please, please. Finn? Finn, are you dead? Oh, don't be dead. Dammit, O'Casey, speak to me!"

Finn groaned and opened his eyes. He lifted his arms and pressed his hands to his head.

"Finn?"

"Guess what, McGee?" he said. "That fat, little guy is *not* Santa Claus."

Four

Liberty insisted that Finn allow her to help him walk back to The Book Mark. She wrapped an arm around his waist, draped one of his arms over her shoulders, and they started off. You had to be very careful, she said adamantly, when you had suffered a severe blow to the head.

Finn, who by then had nothing more than a dull headache, opened his mouth to protest, then snapped it closed. Cat O'Casey had not raised a fool for a son.

"Are you dizzy?" she asked anxiously as they walked.

"What? Oh, no, no. I'm fine."

"You don't have to be macho for me, Finn."

"Thank you, Miss Marple," he said solemnly. "You're most kind."

They walked in silence for another block.

"Finn, why is it that you, a painter, can quote literature like a pro?"

"It was an ongoing contest that Tabor and I played with Cat at dinner. He loved to read, especially classics. He'd whip out a quote and try to trip us up. When he was away, Tabor and I would search through the volumes in his library trying to find something he wouldn't recognize."

Liberty laughed in delight. "Did you ever beat him?"

Lord, how he loved her laugh, Finn thought. "Nope, we never did. And it went on for many years. Tabor and I came to appreciate the masters of the written word. What Cat started as a game with his children turned out to be a precious gift of learning. I hope to do that for my children someday."

She looked up at him in surprise. "You want children? A wife and family?"

Had he actually said that? Finn wondered. Yes, he had. Maybe he'd hit his head harder than he thought. He'd long ago put the idea of a family on a back shelf in his mind, knowing his physical and emotional energies had to be centered on his art if he was to succeed.

But he hadn't known about the loneliness.

He was a success, but that didn't mean he could produce less than top-quality work in the future. He could lighten up on his schedule, though, put some balance in his life now, like his agent had said. Start living a little. Did he want a family who would be waiting for him when he emerged from the studio? Yes, he did. He truly did.

And until that very moment, walking along the filthy sidewalk with Liberty nestled against him, he hadn't realized it.

"Finn?"

"Yes, I'd like a wife and family," he said gruffly. "Someday. Do you want a husband and children?"

"Yes," she said softly. "Someday."

They walked another block in silence, then Liberty sighed.

"Finn? Clarence Smith was acting out a role, wasn't he? That probably isn't even his real name. Those papers I signed for The Book Mark were phony."

"Do you have copies of those papers?"

"Yes."

"I know someone in the records and deeds department at City Hall. I'll make a call when we get back to your apartment and find out for certain."

"Do you think you should see a doctor about your head?"

He chuckled. "No. A couple of aspirin will fix me up as good as new."

"Clarence Smith was so nice to me, so sweet, just like . . ."

"Santa Claus. Yeah, so you said."

"And he whopped you on the head with a wastebasket." She clicked her tongue. "That was very rude of him. Just terrible."

"Well," Finn said slowly, "he didn't actually slamdunk my head with that thing. He sort of flipped it behind him and I . . . Well, I fell over it. I did an Olympic-form dive and landed on the floor. That's . . . um, how I hit my head." He slid her a quick glance out of the corner of his eye.

"You *fell* over the wastebasket?"

"Hey, let's not get picky here about wounds sustained in combat. I do have a helluva goose egg on the back of my head, you know."

"I wonder if Spenser ever fell over a wastebasket and clobbered his head?" Liberty mused, staring off into space.

"Mmm," Finn said, frowning.

In Liberty's apartment, Finn took two aspirin, then reached for the telephone book. Liberty produced the papers she had signed in Clarence Smith's office. After what seemed an eternity to her, Finn thanked the person he was speaking to and replaced the receiver.

"Well?" Liberty asked, sitting down next to him on the sofa.

"Interesting. Clarence Smith is a registered attorney in the state of California. These papers are legal, have been assigned a new deed and title number, and The Book Mark is in the process of being officially transferred into your name. You definitely own the store and this apartment."

"That means that if Aunt Beverly left on her own she has no intention of coming back." Liberty's eyes widened. "Oh, Finn, that also means that if someone forced her to go, they have no intention of allowing her to return."

He nodded. "Think about this though. People who snatch other people don't give a tinker's damn about the snatchee's personal business. When Mickey Mason's muscle grabbed me, they didn't care if I'd left the water running in my bathtub, or my house unlocked, or whatever. Snatchers just snatch."

"Your jargon is awesome, Fletch," Liberty said, rolling her eyes.

"You're being picky again. Do you understand my point? This is looking more and more like a carefully executed plan by someone who cared what happened to The Book Mark."

"Aunt Beverly."

"Bingo. I'm betting that she's alive and well, Keats is with her, and she knows her pride and joy, the store, is in good hands."

"But why fake her own death?"

"That, Lord Peter Wimsey, I don't know."

"I think we're going to run out of detectives' names before we solve this riddle," she said dismally. "None of this makes sense."

The telephone rang, and Finn picked up the receiver and handed it to Liberty.

"Hello?"

"Miss Shaw? This is Victoria Manfield. Do you have my package?"

Liberty looked at Finn and wrinkled her nose. "No, I'm sorry, Miss Manfield, I haven't had a chance to look yet. I've been terribly busy. I'll start right now."

"See that you do, young woman. It's imperative that I have my property returned to me. I'll call you in an hour, and I expect to hear that my package is ready for me to pick up."

"But . . . Well . . . Miss Manfield?" Liberty handed the phone back to Finn. "She hung up on me. She expects me to have the package ready for her when she calls back in an hour."

Finn replaced the receiver and stood up. "So,

let's find it. We have enough on our plate without Miss Money bugging us every two seconds."

Liberty stood as well. "How can I thank you for all you're doing to help me, Finn? I'd be a basket case by now if you weren't here."

He looked at her for a long moment before he spoke. "There's nowhere else I want to be. We're in this together, Liberty."

"Thank you."

"Enough of that. I'll start in this room, you take the bedroom. Go." He brushed his lips over hers. "Pretend you're on a treasure hunt."

"Mmm," she said, and went off to the bedroom.

Finn watched her go, then opened the closet and began looking for Victoria Manfield's package.

In the bedroom, Liberty started carefully going through the dresser drawers. Finn's words echoed in her mind.

We're in this together, Liberty.

In *this* together, she mused. *This* being the mystery surrounding Aunt Beverly. And then what? Would Finn say, "Thanks for the adventure, kid. It was a real kick. See ya," and disappear from her life? Well, of course, he'd go when the riddle was solved. And she'd go, too, at summer's end, back to Chicago. That would be that.

She opened another drawer. But what about Finn's insistence that they solve the riddle of what was happening between them? What about the "go with the flow"? The kisses they'd shared? What if . . . what if the new, strange pull they felt toward each other was the beginning, the stirring, the first flicker . . . of love?

"Don't be silly," she said, slamming the drawer shut. She yanked open another one. She wasn't falling in love with Finn any more than he was falling in love with her. Of course not. They were . . . strongly attracted to each other. But the thought of Finn waving a breezy good-bye and walking out of her life made her stomach hurt. And her heart hurt.

No, no, no, Liberty thought, going to the closet. She would not, could not, fall in love with Finn O'Casey. The wondrous, glorious sensations and feelings that flowed through her when Finn held and kissed her would not be allowed to matter. She would return to Chicago with memories, lovely memories, and nothing more.

What was happening between her and Finn?

She didn't want to know.

She didn't want to deal with the answer.

Because if it turned out she was falling in love with Finn, she'd go back to Chicago with a broken heart.

With a sigh, Liberty closed the closet door, then dropped to her knees to peer under the bed.

Where in the blue blazes was Victoria Manfield's package?

"Yes, I know you've called every hour for the last five hours, Miss Manfield," Liberty said. "We've just finished going through the last of the boxes in the store. Believe me, we conducted a very thorough search. There is no package with your name on it in the bookstore, or here in the apartment. I'm sorry."

"Sorry!" Victoria practically screamed. "You can't simply say you're sorry and consider this a closed issue. I must have that package."

"I can't produce something that isn't here," Liberty said wearily. "I don't know what my aunt Beverly did with it."

"Tell her to put a cork in it," Finn said, sprawling into a chair. "The package isn't here, for Pete's sake."

"Miss Manfield," Liberty said, striving for patience, "there's no purpose in discussing this further. Saying it over and over isn't going to change anything."

"But . . . there must be somewhere else you can look. You don't understand, Miss Shaw. That book is . . . Please, think. Are you sure you checked everywhere?"

"Positive."

"But what could have happened to it?" Victoria asked, sounding close to tears.

"I really have no idea," Liberty said. Unless . . . Aunt Beverly took it with her for some unknown reason. "I really don't."

"Yes, yes, I believe you. Oh my Lord, what am I going to do? Thank you, Miss Shaw, I—I must go. Good-bye."

"Good-bye," Liberty said to the dial tone. "She's terribly upset, Finn," she said, plopping the receiver into place. "She's really coming unglued. Finn, what if Aunt Beverly took that package with her when she left here?"

"What for?"

Liberty threw up her hands. "I don't know.

There's so much I don't know right now it's disgraceful. Oh, I'm exhausted and filthy from plowing through all those boxes of books."

"Me, too, chief," Finn said, pushing himself to his feet. "I'm heading home for a shower and clean clothes. Are you going to be all right here alone? This has been a rather unsettling day. Not exactly ordinary, that's for sure."

Finn O'Casey's kisses weren't ordinary either, Liberty thought, looking up at him. Heavens, the man was gorgeous even when he was covered in grime. She didn't want him to leave. Not now. Not tonight. Not ever? No, she wasn't going to think. She was too tired to think.

"I'll be fine, Finn. I'm too pooped to worry about anything."

He extended his hand to her. "Up, my lady. You've got to follow me downstairs and lock up good behind me."

She placed her hand in his and instantly felt the now familiar heat, the now familiar strength, and the now familiar gentleness.

He drew her up and pulled her close, and kissed her until she was trembling.

"Gotta go," he said, his lips still against hers. "Now."

"Yes."

"I don't want to leave you, but I have to. If I stay . . . No, I'm going. I'll be back in the morning."

"Yes."

"I want you, Liberty. I want to make love to you so damn bad, I ache."

"I—"

"No, don't say anything. It's too soon, too fast, I know that." He stared up at the ceiling for a long moment, then met her gaze again. "But a part of me says it isn't too soon at all, that we've come so far so quickly, it's as though I've known you for a lifetime. Forget it. I'm not even making sense to myself." He dropped his arms and stepped back. "Come on. Let's go downstairs."

At the front door to the store, he brushed his thumb over her lips. "I'm not going to kiss you again tonight. I'm hanging on by a thread here. I'll see you tomorrow."

"All right, Finn," she said softly. "Sleep well."

He chuckled. "I doubt it. 'Bye."

He left the store and waited until he heard the lock snap into place, then started walking slowly down the sidewalk.

He did not, he realized, want to go home to that huge, empty house in Beverly Hills. He'd grown up in that house. When he was twenty-two he'd had one wing remodeled to include his studio. He lived there, while Tabor had lived in her wing until she'd married Jared, and Cat in his until he'd died. There were good memories of loving times within the walls of that home.

But tonight the house waiting for him seemed too big and echoing, empty and lonely.

"Hell," he muttered, slowing his step even more.

Liberty stood in the shower and shampooed her hair, relishing the feel of the hot water beating against her aching muscles. As she dried with a pink and blue polka-dot towel, she blanked her mind and refused to think. About anything. Or anyone.

She ate a jelly sandwich, drank a glass of milk, and turned out the lights, already envisioning cool sheets and the soft pillow on the bed. She made her way carefully across the dark living room, determined not to bump into any of the multitude of boxes.

Suddenly she stopped and snapped her head around toward the curtained window.

The man, she thought. She'd forgotten all about him. Was he there? Was he watching? She didn't want to know. She had to know.

Her heart thudded painfully as she crept forward, and her hands were shaking when she gripped the drapes. She took a steadying breath, then parted the material enough to peer out with one eye.

"Oh, no," she whispered. "He's there. Oh, he's there again and I'm so scared. He's watching me. Watching me. Finn, I need you. I need you, Finn."

Wearing only jeans, his hair still damp from his shower, Finn finished the last of three tuna sandwiches, drained the soda can, then wandered into the living room. His bare feet sank into the rust-colored carpet as he strode over to the sofa.

Propping his feet on the coffee table, he pressed the remote control button for the television, turning it on. He changed from one channel to the next before he could comprehend what he was seeing, then turned the TV off. The screen became dark, leaving only a white dot in the center that stared at him like a disapproving eye before disappearing.

Finn stood up, realized he had no particular destination in mind, and with a sigh of disgust, sprawled back onto the sofa. The restlessness plaguing him was unusual, and he didn't like it.

The big house seemed to echo the sound of his beating heart. The familiar rooms did not wrap him in their usual comforting blanket of welcome, but instead mocked him with the fact that he was alone in the great expanse.

Alone and lonely.

The image of Liberty danced before his eyes. Beautiful, beautiful Liberty.

Finn glanced around, imagining Liberty in the room, her dark eyes sparkling, her rich, husky laughter bouncing off the walls and filling the area with a warmth that was now missing. His memory taunted him with remembrances of her lips moving beneath his, of her full breasts crushed to his chest, of her entire slender body against his. Heat gathered within him, stirring his manhood, and he shifted uncomfortably on the sofa.

Never before had he wanted to make love to a woman with the driving need that he had for Liberty.

Their joining would be special, different. It would be beyond description in its ecstasy. It would combine the emotional with the physical for the first time in his life, because it would be with Liberty.

Finn's feet hit the floor with a muffled thud, and he stiffened, sitting bolt upright.

Dear Lord, he thought, was he falling in love with Liberty Shaw?

"No, now, hey, calm down, O'Casey," he said and surged to his feet.

He began to pace, roaming back and forth like a caged animal. He was being held captive by his inner turmoil, the question beating against his brain.

Was he falling in love with Liberty Shaw?

Finn mentally threw up his hands. Well, hell, how was he supposed to know? He'd skittered around and away from love for so long, he wasn't sure he'd recognize it if it hit him with a two-by-four. Tucker Boone and Nick Capoletti had known love from the moment they'd opened their arms and hearts to Alison and Pippa. Jared Loring had stormed along in a crabby fog, wondering what his problem was, until Tabor had had enough and made him realize he was in love with her. Different strokes for different folks, apparently, when dealing with love.

And Finn O'Casey? he asked himself.

Finn O'Casey was a confused mess.

Wonderful.

"Dammit, Liberty," he said, "you're driving me nuts." He'd had enough of this for one night, he decided. He'd go to bed, get some sleep, and hope to the heavens that things would be clearer and make some sense in the light of the new day. Not only did he have to figure out what was happening to *him*, he had to start solving the riddle concerning Bev.

He reached out to turn off the lamp, then hesitated as his glance fell on the telephone.

He'd hated to leave Liberty alone in that apartment above The Book Mark. Maybe, he mused, he should call her, make sure she was all right, ask her if she was positive she'd locked the place up good and tight. But what if she was already in bed? In bed. Wearing what? Her silken auburn hair would be spread out on the pillow, her chocolate brown eyes would darken with desire as he lay beside her. . . .

He groaned. "Dammit, O'Casey. Would you please knock it off?"

He yanked open the drawer in the end table, pulled out the telephone book, and whacked it onto the table. He flipped through the pages, tearing a few as he went, then found the listing for The Book Mark. As he dialed the number he had a sinking feeling in the pit of his stomach that hearing Liberty's voice was going to make him even more aware of just how big, and empty, and lonely, his house—and bed—really were.

"Yes? Hello?"

"Liberty? Finn. I just wondered—"

"Oh, Finn, thank God you called. Yell at me, tell me I'm acting ridiculous, dumb, and stupid. Please? Okay? Say all that right now."

"Liberty, what is it? What's wrong?"

"The man is out there again, Finn," she said, her voice trembling. "He's across the street in the shadows, and he's watching me. No, he's not. He's looking at the stars, right? He goes for a walk, then he stops and—"

"Dammit, I forgot all about him. Liberty, listen to me. Just stay put with the lights off. Don't move, understand? I'm on my way, but don't open the door until you're positive it's me. Got that?"

"Yes, but I can't ask you to come all the way back here just because I'm acting like a scared child."

"You're not asking me, I'm telling you. I'm on my way." He slammed down the phone and ran toward his bedroom for shoes and a shirt.

Where were the cops when a guy was driving like a maniac? Finn wondered as he ran another red light. Wherever they were, he prayed they stayed there. He had to get to Liberty. She was frightened and alone, she needed him, and he was going to her because that was where he belonged.

Was he falling in love with Liberty Shaw?

"Not now, O'Casey. Give it a rest."

Posh turned into poverty as Finn entered the neighborhood of The Book Mark. He parked on a side street a block away from the store, then strode quickly along the sidewalk, staying in the shadows of the buildings.

And then he saw him.

Directly across the street from the bookstore, a short, stocky man was barely visible in the shadowy light cast by the streetlamp twenty feet away. The man's head was tilted back, as though to give him a clear view of the front window of Liberty's apartment.

Or was he looking at the stars? Finn wondered, feeling sweat trickle down his back. There was only one way to find out. Ask him.

It took Finn nearly fifteen minutes to retrace his steps, go around the block behind the bookstore, cross the street, and creep down the alley. There was a cut-through from the alley to the sidewalk one building over from where the man stood. Finn peered around the corner of the grimy building and saw the man hadn't moved.

Finn silently inched his way forward, mentally drawing on everything Cat O'Casey had ever taught him.

Ten more steps . . . eight . . . six . . . four . . . two . . .

In one smooth motion, Finn closed the remaining distance, wrapped a forearm around the thick neck of the man, and grabbed his shirtfront with his other hand.

"What in the hell—"

"Take it easy," Finn said. The guy was solid as a rock, he realized, muscle from head to toe. Finn was a lot taller, but was outweighed by at least forty pounds of what felt like a body made of bricks. Wonderful. "Just answer one question and nobody gets hurt." He hoped. "Why are you watching the apartment above The Book Mark?"

"Who wants to know?" the man asked gruffly.

"*I* do," Finn said, tightening his hold on the man's throat. "Now."

"Buzz off, kid. I never said I was watching that apartment."

"I think you are, and I want to know why." The man strained against Finn's hold, and Finn's muscles protested from the pressure. "I don't want to hurt you, small size," he said. How corny, he thought. Would Spenser say something like that? "Just answer the question."

"Who are you?" the man asked.

For Pete's sake, Finn thought, did people formally introduce themselves in situations like this? Oh, what the hell, what did he know? "Finn O'Casey."

"O'Casey? *O'Casey*?"

"Do you have a hearing problem? Yeah, O'Casey."

"Ever heard of Cat O'Casey?" the man asked.

"Dammit, mister, I'm not here for a family reunion. Cat was my father. Okay? Happy now? Start telling me what you're doing watching that apartment, and don't say you're not, because I know you are. Spit it out, hot dog." Not bad, Finn thought. That had sounded mean, lean, and tough. Maybe.

"Cat's kid," the man said. "I'll be damned." He stopped straining against Finn's hold. "Your old man was the best there was. Could he scale a building. I miss him. We all do. Lighten up, kid, you're wrinkling my shirt."

Finn dropped his arms and stepped back, wondering in the next instant if that had been a stupid thing to do. If the joker broke his face, he'd know it had not been a swift move. Having had Cat *tell* him what to do was sure different from on-the-job training.

The man smoothed his shirt, probed his neck with one hand, then turned to face Finn. He appeared to be in his early fifties.

"Yeah, you're Cat's kid, all right," he said. "I can see the resemblance. I heard you were an artist or something. What are you doing on the streets?"

"Wondering why you're watching that apartment."

"What's it to you?"

"You're scaring the hell out of the young woman who's in there."

"She your lady?"

"I . . . Yeah, she's my lady," Finn said, crossing his arms over his chest.

"Don't stand like that, kid. I could sucker-punch you in the belly so fast you'd never know what train hit you."

"Oh." Finn dropped his arms back to his sides.

"Look, O'Casey, you're crossing the line into Cat's old turf, and you don't belong here. Go paint a picture."

"Now wait just a damn minute. I—"

"Son," the man said in an unexpectedly gentle voice, "your father saved my life once. I owe him. I didn't know that was your lady up there. I'm just doing my job."

"What job?"

"Making sure nobody hassles her. Now it looks like I'll have to keep your tail out of the fire too. You're not exactly Joe Slick on the streets, boy. By the way, my name is Crusher."

"I don't think I'll ask why you're called that."

"Heard tell Jared Loring married your sister."

"Yeah."

"Loring was some kind of agent. Top-of-the-line, state-of-the-art. Hated to see him retire like he did."

"Look . . . Crusher, I'm really enjoying chatting with you, but it's not getting me any answers. Who might want to hassle Liberty Shaw?"

Crusher shrugged. "Maybe somebody, maybe nobody. I'm making sure it's nobody. She should be okay, totally out of this, but you never know."

"Out of what?"

"Can't tell you that, kid."

"What if I told you I think Bev Shaw is alive."

"She croaked."

"The hell she did," Finn said. "She packed up and left, even took her cat with her. I thought at first she might have been snatched, but I changed my mind. I figure she set it all up nice and tidy, making sure Liberty got the store. Then she faked her own death and disappeared. Why?"

"You know too much as it is," Crusher said. "Cat would be proud of the way you've pieced it together, but you're walking straight into trouble if you don't leave it alone. Your lady is safe, she's got a nice little store there. Let it go, kid. Keep your O'Casey nose out of this. Nothing will happen to you, or the girl, if you just go about your business as usual."

"Come on, Crusher, give me something. What in the hell is going on?"

"No can do, and you know it too. I can't believe that Cat's kid doesn't know *anything* about how this stuff goes down. Look, just don't make waves. This should be wrapped up pretty quick, if nothing gets screwed up. Get off the street, O'Casey, and let me do my job."

"Well, hell."

"Trust me."

"Oh, yeah, sure. You're protecting Liberty, and I got the jump on you. That really does wonderful things for my peace of mind."

Crusher sighed and shook his head. "Finn, Finn, you never had me. I watched you skulking along in the shadows across the street, then you went around the block, and came down the cut-through. I decided to find out who sent you before I broke your ribs. That's why I let you dance me around at first. Believe it, kid, your lady is safe."

"Oh." For the life of him Finn couldn't think of another thing to say. Spenser would not be impressed.

"Go calm your lady down," Crusher said.

"Yeah, okay."

"See ya. Oh, and Finn?"

"Yeah?"

"Your dad was a helluva man."

"Thanks, Crusher. Good night."

"Yep."

Finn sprinted across the street and pounded on the door to The Book Mark.

Liberty gasped and jumped when she heard the loud knocking below on the front door. Was it Finn? she wondered.

Her eyes had long since grown accustomed to the darkness. She'd been sitting stiffly on the sofa, her hands clutched tightly in her lap. The minutes had dragged by with agonizing slowness as she'd waited for Finn.

She slowly stood up, crossed the room, and opened the apartment door. The noise of the knocking was immediately louder. Swallowing heavily, she made her way down the narrow staircase. In the bookstore, the pounding was so thunderous, she envisioned the door splintering under the impact. Her heart raced painfully fast.

"Who is it?" she called.

"Finn. Open up."

"How do I know you're really Finn?"

"Because I said so. Liberty, it's me. Finn O'Casey. Open the door."

"But I can't be sure it's you. Say something Finny."

"Finny?"

"Yes, something Finn would say. I'm not opening that door, bub, until I'm convinced you're Finn O'Casey."

"Okay, listen up. 'I am the master of my fate; I am the captain of my soul.' How's that?"

"William Ernest Henley. Oh, Finn, it's you." She unlocked the door and flung it open. In the next instant she was plastered against him, wrapping her arms tightly around his neck.

He chuckled. "I'm glad to see you, too, but I think we should close and lock the door."

"Oh, yes, yes, of course. Thank you for coming, Finn. I just couldn't handle any more tonight, and when I looked out the window and saw that man watching me again, I just—"

"Shh. Calm down. There, the door is locked. Let's go upstairs and I'll fill you in."

In Liberty's living room, Finn swept his gaze over Liberty. She was wearing only a nightshirt with Shakespeare's picture on the front.

"Lucky old Bill," he said.

"Heavens, I'm not even dressed."

"Don't worry about it. You wouldn't be that covered up if we were on a beach. Sit." He sat down on the sofa and tugged on her hand. She sat close to him. "All right, here's what happened outside." What did she have on underneath that thing? he wondered. No, he didn't dare think about that now. "I saw the guy across the street and . . ."

Liberty's gaze was riveted on Finn's face as he told her what had happened with Crusher. The only part he left out was Crusher's announcement that Finn's skulking had been less than wonderful and that his ribs were intact because Crusher had decided they should be. A man, Finn rationalized, did have his pride.

"That's the scoop," he said finally. Lord, he thought. The soft material of that nightshirt was clinging so seductively to Liberty's breasts. "End of report."

"You took a terrible risk grabbing Crusher like that."

"Not . . . really. Just forget that part. Crusher is one of the good guys, Liberty, and I'm glad he's out there because we really don't know any more than we did before, except that government agents are involved. Bev is alive, I'm positive of it. Beyond that? Nada. Crusher wouldn't tell me a thing."

"Well, darn it, this is frustrating. They really expect us to go merrily about our business and pretend nothing weird is happening?"

"Yep."

"Are we going to follow those orders?"

"Nope."

"Oh, good. What do we do next, Fletch?"

"You're awfully brave again all of a sudden."

"Well, you're here, and I have a bodyguard named Crusher. Is that really his name?"

"Don't ask."

"Okay. So? Speak."

"Tonight we get some sleep. Then tomorrow . . ."

"Yes?" she asked, raising her eyebrows. "Tomorrow?"

"I'll call Jared Loring."

Five

Finn shifted again on the lumpy sofa in Liberty's living room in another attempt to find a comfortable position. He failed miserably. The sofa, he deduced, was not fit for man or beast.

That he was sentenced to sleeping on that instrument of torture was his own fault. Even though Crusher was solidly in place across the street, Finn had been determined not to leave Liberty alone for the remainder of the night. It hadn't made sense even to him, since he knew Crusher was thoroughly capable of watching over Liberty. Finn also knew that it would have taken a gun being pointed at his head to get him to walk out that door.

Neither wishing to sound totally insane, nor wanting to lessen Liberty's faith in her newly discovered Crusher-the-bodyguard, Finn had pleaded a worsening headache and mind-boggling fatigue. Liberty had fluttered and fussed over him, and he'd enjoyed every minute of her attention. He would, she had insisted, sleep right there on the sofa and not even consider making the grueling drive back to Beverly Hills.

Finn had thrown up his hands in feigned defeat, then given Liberty what he now realized had been a rather sappy smile.

And then he'd nearly died. He'd sat in a chair and clenched his jaw until it ached as he watched Liberty bend and stretch this way and that, tucking sheets onto the crummy sofa. He'd caught a glimpse of lace on the edge of her panties at the top of those long, long satiny legs that disappeared beneath the nightshirt, and saw Shakespeare's face shift and move over her firm breasts.

He could still feel the throbbing heat low in his body as he lay beneath the top sheet, wearing only his briefs. Liberty was a room away, a few short feet, and he ached with the want of her. He'd managed to give her a quick kiss good night, praying she wouldn't see the evidence of his arousal pressing against his jeans, or his hands curled into tight fists to keep from hauling her into his arms.

He'd nearly sighed aloud with relief when she had trotted off to bed, then inwardly groaned because she'd left her door wide open. Now, an hour later, he was cursing the lousy sofa as well as himself for subjecting his poor body to such total misery. Between the spring that was poking him in the back and the heat pulsing within him, he was a dying man. And to top it off, the headache he'd faked was now a painful reality. Hell.

The headache, Finn decided, he could do something about. Liberty kept the aspirin in the kitchen cupboard, and if he could get that far without killing himself tripping over the boxes of books, he could remedy at least one of his problems.

He sat up, looked at the dark cave of a bedroom that contained Liberty, then got to his feet. Squinting into the darkness, he cautiously crossed the room, arriving at last in the small kitchen. He turned on the light and hoped it wouldn't sneak around the corner and wake Liberty. The aspirin were where he thought they were, and he took two with a tall glass of cool water.

Now, maybe, although he had his serious doubts, he'd be able to sleep. He turned from the counter, then stopped dead.

Liberty was standing in the kitchen doorway.

Liberty, in her soft, clinging nightshirt with Bill's face on the front. Liberty, with her wavy auburn hair in sensual disarray. Liberty, with those long, satiny legs and full breasts. Liberty, whose dark eyes were filled with concern. Liberty was standing in the doorway.

Finn's heart started to beat wildly, and he swallowed as he felt the rush of heat pounding low within him. He searched his mind frantically for something witty to say, something that would have made Spenser beam with pride, but came up empty. He simply looked at Liberty.

Dear heaven, Liberty thought, Finn. Magnificent Finn. His bare chest was tanned, covered in tawny curls, and broad and strong. Before he'd realized she was there she'd scrutinized all of him, every inch. He'd stood in profile to her, and she'd seen the strength of his tanned legs, the smattering of white-blond hair on them, the tightness of his buttocks clad only in snug underwear that rode low on his narrow hips.

And then he'd turned, their eyes had met, and she now felt pinned in place, unable to move . . . or breathe. She knew there was a warm flush on her cheeks, and also knew it was caused by the desire thrumming deep inside her.

Finn had awakened within her all that was woman, and she rejoiced in her newly discovered femininity, for she was the counterpart to Finn, the man. Her breasts were suddenly heavy, sensitive, the soft cotton nightshirt abrasive against the tender flesh. Her heart was beating rapidly, her skin was tingling, and she inhaled his aroma of soap and the earthy scent of simply him.

This was Finn O'Casey. And she wanted to make love with him.

She knew this moment was real, and right, and meant to be. Regrets would be born only from denying what had been destined from the instant she'd seen Finn standing in a halo of sunshine.

Oh, yes, she wanted to make love with Finn because she was falling in love with him. The idea of loving Finn wasn't frightening, she realized. She was wrapped in the safe cocoon of night, where the glaring truths and bright, revealing light of tomorrow could not enter. There was only now. And Finn.

"Finn," she said softly, then gently smiled.

Her whisper seemed to float over Finn, stroking him, heightening his desire, causing the blood to pound in his veins. The room faded into oblivion, and he saw only Liberty standing before him. One thought pushed past the jumbled confusion in his mind and stood alone, strong, and true, and all-consuming.

He was in love with Liberty Shaw.

The chill of loneliness within him was quelled by the warmth of love and the building heat of passion.

He loved her.

"Liberty," he said, his voice husky. "Come here."

He opened his arms to her, and she came.

With a soft sigh of pleasure and a sense of completeness, Liberty moved into Finn's embrace, wrapping her arms around his waist. She felt his powerful arms enfold her, and he pulled her close to his heated body. She tilted her head back to meet his smoldering gaze, and knew the desire in his brown eyes was matched by the desire in hers.

"If I kiss you now," he said, "I won't be able to stop. I want you, Liberty. I want to make love with you. *With* you, knowing you want this to happen as much as I do."

"Yes, Finn, I want you too," she said, her voice not quite steady. "I truly do."

"No regrets later? I couldn't handle it if you were sorry, if you wished you hadn't given yourself to me. I realize we haven't known each other long, but . . . but we really have. It's been a lifetime. It's . . ." He shook his head. "I'm not saying this very well." He loved her. Loved her! He was in love for the first time, for all time, but he couldn't say it now. It would sound phony, like a declaration he hoped would tip the scale and get her into his bed. "I have to be certain that you have no doubts."

"Oh, no, Finn, no doubts," she said. No doubts, no fears, only love. She loved Finn O'Casey. But she couldn't tell him of her love now. She couldn't run the risk of breaking the glorious spell of this night with words he didn't want to hear. This night was theirs. "I want to make love *with* you. Now, Finn? Please?"

With a groan, he brought his mouth down hard on hers. His tongue parted her lips and he tasted her sweetness. His hands roamed over her back, then pulled up her nightshirt to gain access to her buttocks covered in the scrap of lace and satin panties. He spread his legs slightly to press her to his throbbing arousal, the cradle of his hips fitting hers perfectly. He tore his mouth from hers.

"Liberty," he said, his breathing rough, "let's go into the bedroom before it's too late. Oh, Lord, how I want you. I've never, ever, wanted anyone the way I do you. Come on."

"Yes."

He snapped off the kitchen light, and they made their way through the cluttered living room by the glow of the small lamp next to the bed. The simply furnished bedroom had a rosy hue cast over it, a welcoming warmth.

Standing next to the bed, Finn cradled Liberty's face in his hands and looked directly into her eyes. As hearts raced and passions soared, they gazed at each other, drinking in the sight of the one each knew they loved. But neither said the words as they waited for a better time to speak the message from their hearts and souls.

Finn dipped his head and ran his tongue lightly

over Liberty's lips, back and forth, as though savoring the nectar of a delicate flower. She trembled, the feathery foray causing whispers of heat to curl deep within her, then burst into a raging flame.

"Finn, oh, please."

He lifted his head and drew the nightshirt up and away, dropping it onto the floor. His hands shaking, he cupped her breasts, his thumbs stroking the nipples to taut points.

"Beautiful. You're exquisite, Liberty, like ivory velvet." His voice was harsh with passion.

Slowly, he slid his hands down her sides. He skimmed her panties along her legs, and she stepped free of them. In the next instant he removed his shorts, and they stood naked before each other, unafraid, yearning.

"And you are beautiful too," Liberty said, her gaze sweeping over his magnificent, aroused body.

He lifted her onto the cool sheets, then stretched out next to her, kissing her deeply before seeking the lush bounty of her breasts. He drew one nipple into his mouth, laving it with his tongue as his fingers teased the other nipple. Then his hand caressed lower in unhurried pleasure over her dewy skin. Then lower yet to seek and find her femininity that held such promise of ecstasy to come.

Liberty splayed one hand on Finn's back, feeling his moist, warm skin and his muscles bunching and moving beneath her palm. She sank her other fingers into his thick hair, urging his mouth harder onto her breast. As his hand found the heat of her womanhood, her body seemed to sing with sensual joy, the blood humming through her veins like liquid fire.

An artist's hands, she thought dreamily. Strong but gentle hands. Finn's hands, that created beauty on canvas and made her feel beautiful by their mere touch. It was as though he were painting her image in his mind as he caressed her. Oh, how she loved him, wanted him, needed him. Now.

"Finn . . ." she cried softly.

He left her breast and his mouth swept down onto hers, his questing tongue stroking hers in the same rhythm as his sweetly torturing fingers.

"So ready for me," he murmured against her lips. "You want me as much as I want you."

"Yes, oh, yes. Please, Finn. Come to me."

He moved over her, catching his weight on his forearms, his muscles trembling from forced restraint. He kissed her once more, then lifted his head to watch her face as he entered her with smooth power, filling her, bringing to her honeyed haven all that he was as a man.

A gasp of pleasure escaped her as she received Finn into her body, sealing forever the unspoken vow of love in her heart. They were one. This was a meshing of bodies, and senses, and souls.

Finn began to move within her, slowly at first, then increasing the tempo. She matched it eagerly, lifting her hips to meet him, to allow him to drive deeper into her, as the thundering cadence carried them up and away from reality. Currents of tension swept through her, tightening, churning, coiling with pulsing heat.

"Finn," she said, gripping his shoulders.

"Yes. Now. Yes. I'm right here. Now, Liberty!"

"Finn!"

Her body surged upward as she felt the waves of

ecstasy sweep her to a place of shattering pleasure. An instant later, Finn threw back his head
and called her name as he shuddered above her,
tumbling after her into the abyss. He collasped
against her, spent, his skin glistening in the glow
of the lamp.

Never, he thought hazily, had he experienced
anything so incredibly beautiful, so total, so inti-
mate. But never before had he loved. More than
his seed of life had passed from him into Liberty.
He had given her his soul, his love for all time. He
would never let her go. She was his.

"Liberty?" he said, raising his head and shift-
ing his weight onto his arms. "Are you all right?"

She opened her eyes and met his gaze. "Oh,
yes. It was so wonderful, so . . ." Her voice trailed
off.

"Yes." He brushed his lips over hers, then moved
carefully from her, reaching for the sheet to cover
their cooling bodies. "Yes, it was."

She put her head on his shoulder and rested her
hand on his chest.

"No regrets?" he asked, gently stroking her back.

"Never. This night will be a precious memory."

Precious memory, he thought. To take back to
Chicago with her? To remember when she exam-
ined her do-something-different summer? Well, he
had news for Miss Liberty Shaw. Finn O'Casey
had no intention of being just a memory that
would fade in time and be replaced by another. He
could provide the stability and permanence she
needed in her life. She had no reason to cling to
Chicago and her existence there. They'd create a
world of their own. A forever world. Together.

She yawned, and he chuckled.

"Go to sleep," he said. He reached beyond her and turned off the light. "Go to sleep, my love."

" 'Kay," she said, closing her eyes.

My love, her mind and heart whispered. If only it were true. If only Finn loved her as she loved him. But she also remembered his adamant stand on not falling prey to his sister's matchmaking schemes. His art, his painting, came first. At the moment, Finn was taking a much needed rest from his work, was indulging in do-something-different time.

But so was she, Liberty thought suddenly. She didn't live here, she belonged in Chicago. She had a contract to teach there in the fall. Her home was there. But the man she loved was here. A man who wanted a wife and family . . . someday. A someday that might never come because Finn's focus was on his painting.

She'd made it clear to him that she intended to stay in Chicago. So be it. She'd have to be careful, she thought sleepily, and neither say nor do anything to give Finn a hint of the depth of her true feelings for him. Do nothing to cut short the precious days she had left with him.

Yes, she'd have to be careful.

And when she returned to Chicago, she'd cry.

Liberty sighed, then gave way to her fatigue, savoring the contented feeling of being held in Finn's arms.

Finn inhaled the fragrant aroma of Liberty's hair again, then shifted to a more comfortable position, keeping her close to his side. Her steady, even breathing told him she was asleep. Asleep in his arms where she belonged.

He stared into the darkness, warning himself that he had to move slowly. He could not, as much as he wanted to, wake Liberty and tell her he loved her. Between the mystery surrounding her aunt's disappearance, and his own appearance in her life, too much had happened to her too quickly. Chicago was, no doubt, holding greater appeal by the moment, with its routine and the things she could count on not to change. No, he mustn't say anything yet about his love for her.

But, he wondered, what did Liberty truly feel for him? She cared, he knew that, or he wouldn't be in that bed with her at that very moment. She was aware that something special had begun to grow between them the moment they met, but had she given it a name? Did she recognize it as love?

He remembered when Tabor had told him she was in love with Jared Loring, but that she wasn't sure how deeply Jared cared for her. Finn had told her to find out exactly what Jared's feelings were. It sure had sounded easy when he'd told his sister that was all she needed to do. Just jump right in there and find the answers she needed. That Tabor had managed to do it seemed like a miracle. Love was, Finn now realized, very, very complicated.

Well, damn, what a mess, he thought, frowning into the darkness. He was in love for the first time in his life, and he couldn't tell the woman how he felt. It was too risky. Liberty had too much to deal with already. So, easy does it, one step at a time.

The bizarre puzzle about Bev Shaw had to be solved. It was standing in the way. He'd talk to Jared, ask him to see what he could find out from his sources of the night, the people from the world Jared and Cat had lived in for so long.

And in the meantime, Finn told himself, he'd stick like glue to Liberty Shaw. He'd watch and listen for any hints about how she really felt about him. He wouldn't let her forget for a minute how special, rare, and beautiful what they had together was. And, he hoped, the lure of Chicago would dim, Liberty would come to see that her future was with him for all time.

Lord, how he loved her, he thought, his hold on her tightening.

But what if Liberty never came to love him? his little voice taunted.

She would, his mind thundered.

Would she? the voice whispered. She clung to Chicago, because her need to be there, to wrap herself in its security was so great. Chicago and all it offered was a mighty foe.

He'd beat it, Finn's mind declared.

With love? came the voice. Where were the guarantees in love? The absolutes? There weren't any, not with love.

He wasn't going to let her go, his mind shot back. He couldn't lose her and face a future of loneliness. Liberty was his.

Was she? the voice asked. Was she really?

With a groan, Finn ran his hand down his face. Enough of this, he thought. He was driving himself crazy. Cat had always said things looked better in the light of the new day.

Finn forced himself to relax his tensed muscles and welcome the edges of sleep that dulled his mind and quieted the nagging little voice in his head. As he drifted off, he realized that for the first time in his life he was falling asleep with the woman he loved held safely in his arms.

"Jared? This is Finn."

"Hey, how are you? Are you still on your emotional high after your show? Those reviews were great, Finn. But I guess we covered all this the other night when Tabor and I talked to you."

"Yeah, I know, I'm not calling about that. In fact, Jared, this is strictly between you and me. No, that's not right. I can't ask you to keep something from Tabor. I know you two share everything."

"We'll worry about that part later, Finn. You obviously have something serious on your mind."

"Jared, I'm in love," Finn blurted out.

"Tabor would be really tickled with that news flash. Why don't you want your sister to know you've joined the ranks with me, Tucker, and Nick?"

"Because it's so damn complicated. Jared, do you know a guy named Crusher?"

"Sure. He's a good man, tough as they come. The fact that he's getting up in years hasn't slowed him down a bit." Jared paused. "How in the hell do *you* know Crusher?"

"He's my lady's bodyguard, for Pete's sake. I'm telling you, Jared, I'm in the middle of one helluva riddle, and so is Liberty. Liberty Shaw. She's the woman I love. I'm in her apartment now while she's downstairs tending to The Book Mark and—"

"Whoa. Finn, back up here and start over, at the beginning."

"Oh. Okay. Well, whenever I need a break from work I come down to visit my friend Bev Shaw . . ."

Finn told the story to Jared, who listened in silence, not interrupting with questions.

"There you have it," Finn said finally.

"I see," Jared said.

"I'm glad *you* do, because it's a mystery to me, that's for sure. Liberty is caught up in the middle of something and no one is telling us anything. Crusher says to just go about our business and forget it. Fat chance. Jared, I'm convinced Bev Shaw is alive, and this was all carefully worked out. The fact that agents are involved says it's not just an eccentric woman acting on a whim. There's something big going on here."

"Finn, look, Crusher is right. You and Liberty would be better off just staying out of it. Crusher said you'd be safe if you kept out of the way. I know you're Cat O'Casey's son, and you handled yourself well during the mess with Mickey Mason, but you're not a trained agent. You haven't had the experience, despite all that Cat taught you. Why don't you just enjoy being in love and con- centrate on Liberty? Leave this other stuff to the people who know what they're doing."

"No."

Jared sighed. "I didn't think so. I've dealt with the O'Casey stubborn streak more than once with Tabor. Okay, Finn. I'll see what I can find out and get back to you."

"Thanks, Jared."

"Where can I reach you?"

"I'll give you this number. It rings here in Liberty's apartment and in the store downstairs. You have my number at my house, of course."

Finn quickly rattled off Liberty's telephone number.

"Got it," Jared said. "This may take a while. Be patient. And, Finn? Don't start poking around where you don't belong. Checking out Clarence Smith's office and going after Crusher is enough, thank you very much. Believe me, pal, Crusher earned his name. You're lucky he took the time to find out who you were. Are you hearing me, Finn? Stay put."

"Yeah, fine," Finn said gruffly.

"You're pouting because I'm telling you what to do," Jared said, chuckling. "Hey, don't feel bad. You should have heard the lecture Nick got from Pippa's little girl, Emma. Pippa flew to Phoenix with Emma to visit Emma's grandparents. Nick was given strict instructions by a six-year-old about eating right and getting to bed on time, the whole bit. That is one cute kid."

"Yeah, I liked her when I met her at Nick and Pippa's wedding," Finn said, smiling. "They're a nice family."

"Yes, they are. And now the old lovebug has bitten Finn O'Casey. I'm happy for you, Finn. I wouldn't want to be going through life without Tabor. She's in New Orleans for a few days at an antique auction for one of her interior decorating clients. Nick and I are feeling very sorry for ourselves. Being bachelors even for a week is the pits. You should be happy your lady is right where you can see her."

"I'm not certain . . . Well, I love *her*, but she's never said . . . What I mean is . . ."

"Ah. I get the picture. Liberty hasn't actually come out and said that she's in love with *you*. Take it from someone who knows, Finn, love has its own timetable. I was so slow on the uptake it was ridiculous. Thank God Tabor hung in there while I was acting like a jerk. Give your lady some space, all she needs, in fact. You've waited many years for Liberty Shaw, Finn, so she must be very special."

"She is. She really is, Jared."

"Then wait for her to catch up to where you are emotionally. Get the drift?"

"Yes."

Jared laughed. "I sound like I'm an expert on love. I'm not. Your sister still manages to spring surprises on me. Lord, women are terrific creatures. Don't get me started, or I'll end up going to New Orleans and hauling Tabor back here. I miss her like hell." He paused. "As for this other business, I'll get started on it and get back to you when I have something."

"Thanks, Jared, for everything, including the words of wisdom."

"Hang in there, O'Casey."

Jared replaced the receiver, then picked it up again and pressed a number.

"Mrs. Tuttle," a woman answered.

"Hi, love of my life."

"Jared Loring, you're going bonkers with Tabor away. You and Nick both look like lost puppies moping around. As your self-appointed granny, I shall offer my sympathies to you in your hour of need. Oh-h-h, poor you. There, that's it. Now, why are you bothering me? I'm a busy woman."

"You're heartless, that's what you are, Turtle," Jared said. "Have Trig and Spider come up to my office."

"Why?"

"Because I said so! I'm the boss, remember?"

"Big deal. If you want Trig and Spider at the same time, then something is up. What's the scoop? Tell all, Rhett."

"Turtle, you're a pain. Just get them up here."

"Tabor is going to hear about what a grouch you were when she was away. Whoever said that southern boys were always gentlemen was full of—"

"Turtle!"

"Okay, okay, I'll get Trig and Spider. The next time Tabor goes somewhere, I'm going with her."

"Fine. Good-bye," Jared said, then slammed down the phone.

The next time Tabor went somewhere, he thought, *he* was going with her. Lord, he missed that woman. Well, while he was waiting for her to get back, he'd see what he could find out for Finn. Trig and Spider would hit the streets and dig up what they could from the men and women of the night.

Jared leaned back in his leather chair and stared at the ceiling. "Sounds like you're in the middle of a big one, Finn," he said aloud. "Watch your step."

Finn sat in the quiet apartment and replayed in his mind his conversation with Jared. Jared had told him what he already knew. He had to give Liberty time and space. Okay, but he was definitely going to pay attention to what she said and did.

He stood up and started toward the door, stopping as his glance fell on the bedroom doorway. Heat rocketed through his body as he remembered the lovemaking shared with Liberty last night and that morning.

They were fantastic together, he mused. Incredible. They gave and received equally, holding nothing back, reaching heights of passion he hadn't even known existed. He loved Liberty Shaw with an intensity that grew with every passing hour. With her, his life would be complete, *he* would be complete. With her, he would find the proper balance between his dedication to his painting and the warm sunshine created by a family.

And with Liberty, he would never again be lonely.

Six

Liberty knew that a soft gasp of awe and wonder had escaped from her own lips, and made no attempt to stifle the one that followed. She walked slowly forward, her gaze riveted on the next canvas propped against the wall of Finn's studio.

The first two painting she had seen had been beach scenes with waves crashing against the shore during a tempestuous storm. This one was a child shown from the waist up. Her tiny hands were filled with daisies, and her eyes sparkled with anticipation as she looked upward, obviously offering the flowers to someone who was very special to her. The little girl was smiling, her innocence captured forever by Finn's brush. Sunlight poured over her, making her skin and the blond highlights in her curly hair glow. She appeared so real, so alive, that Liberty found herself waiting for the child to speak, to offer the flowers to her.

Unexpected tears misted Liberty's eyes as she

tore her gaze from the painting to look at the next one. She saw the weathered face of an old fisherman, a faded cap on his head, a pipe in his mouth, a stubble of gray beard on his craggy cheeks. His skin was dark and leathery from years of battling the elements, and his eyes held magic. Finn had caught and portrayed the inner peace of the fisherman, the contentment of a man who had spent his life doing what he was meant to do, what had brought him immeasurable joy.

"Oh, Finn," Liberty whispered, dashing an errant tear from her cheek. Such incredible talent he had, she realized. He possessed a gift, a rare and wonderful gift. He'd spent years mastering his craft, devoting himself to his painting, and his work was brilliant. He had not allowed anything or anybody to stand in the way of his goals and dreams. His art had come first, accompanied by the sacrifices and the loneliness, and the rewards of his labor and dedication were his alone to reap.

And, Liberty knew, he must maintain this level of excellence in his work. He would demand it of himself, as would the rest of the world. His focus had to remain on his art.

There wasn't room in his life for love.

There wasn't room for her.

She wrapped her arms around herself and drew a shuddering breath. She loved Finn O'Casey, she thought miserably, but he already had a love, a mistress. His painting. The truth was chilling. She was in love with the wrong man.

She walked toward the floor-to-ceiling windows. A vibrant sunset streaked across the summer sky in rich hues of purple, orange, and yellow. It was as though Finn had lifted his brush and swept the heavens with his masterful touch, creating a spectacle of incredible beauty just for her.

But she knew the sunset was temporary, would soon fade and disappear, and the world would be cloaked in darkness. Temporary, just for now. That was what she was destined to share with Finn. What they had together was as vibrant as the sunset, but when it was over there would be only darkness and loneliness.

Liberty swallowed past the ache of tears in her throat and looked down at the gauzy material of her mint-green dress. Finn had told her she was beautiful in her dress, like a spring flower. They'd driven to his house so he could shower and change, then he'd said he was taking her to a fancy restaurant where he would be the envy of every man who saw her. She'd asked if she could see his studio and he'd complied with a shrug, saying there wasn't much to see due to his recent show.

And so here she was, Liberty thought, in Finn's world, where he created his dreams, spent countless hours achieving his best. Finn's world, which insisted he be there alone, not swayed by the demands of the heart. He wanted a wife and family "someday," but the mistress within this studio would decree that the "someday" would never come.

Liberty was convinced that deep within him, Finn knew that. He grabbed hold of do-something-different time when he was tired and needed to rest, then returned to his world when his mistress called his name. This was where he belonged, and this was where he would stay. Alone.

"Liberty?"

She closed her eyes tightly for a moment to gather her composure and strength, then forced a smile onto her lips as she turned to face Finn.

Magnificent Finn, she thought. In dark slacks, a gray-and-white striped shirt, a gray tie, and a darker gray sport coat, he looked like a model instead of an artist. His thick blond hair shone in the golden hue of the sunset's light. Her fingers itched to smooth over his tanned skin, to trace his handsome features. He was tall and strong, his body as beautiful as a bronzed statue. He was Finn. And she loved him with all that she was.

"These paintings," she said, hearing the slight trembling in her voice, "are wonderful. You're so talented, Finn. Why weren't these in your show?"

He looked at her intently. "I had ones like these. I decided the others were better." He started toward her, moving slowly, still studying her face. "Is something wrong, Liberty?"

"Wrong? Heavens, no. I'm just very moved by what I've seen here. I didn't know quite what to expect, but I realize now that you're someone with a gift. I can understand your dedication to your painting all these years. You have so much to give to people, so much to share."

He stopped in front of her and framed her face in his large hands. "I'm more than an artist, Liberty," he said in a low voice. "I'm a man too. A man with wants, needs, hopes, and dreams, like any other man. My painting is separate from that man." He dipped his head and kissed her lightly. "The artist can be fulfilled in this room. The man still lives with his loneliness."

And that was how it would always be, she thought. Had to be, for Finn.

But not anymore, Finn thought, because now there was Liberty, and he loved her.

"I have never," he said, "kissed a woman in this room. It's time the man meshed with the artist."

"But then the artist," she whispered, looking directly into his eyes, "won't be all he can be."

"He might be even more than he was," he said, then his lips covered hers.

With Finn's hands still cradling her face, Liberty parted her lips to receive his tongue and meet it with her own. She lifted her hands to his broad shoulders as the kiss deepened, crowding her senses and her ability to think. Desire swirled within her as she drank of the taste and aroma of Finn.

A soft sob caught in her throat.

Oh, Liberty, Finn thought hazily. He'd never get enough of her, of her taste, the feel of her soft skin and silken hair. He'd never get enough of making love with her, joining his body with hers, sheathing himself in her warmth that received him so completely, willingly, trustingly. She was his, and he would love her for all time. The artist and the man would always love Liberty Shaw. How he wanted her, now. Ached for her, now. Needed her, now.

He jerked his head up and took a rough breath. "I . . ." He cleared his throat. "I'd better stop kissing you, or we'll never get any dinner."

She slowly opened her eyes. "Dinner?" She paused. "Oh, yes, of course. Yes."

He stroked his thumbs back and forth over her flushed cheeks. She shivered.

"I meant what I said, Liberty. I've never kissed anyone in this studio. It never felt right because . . . I don't know. This is where I paint, where all my concentration has to be on my work. But you fit in this room, Liberty."

"Maybe—maybe that's because you're not painting now. You're indulging in do-something-different time. Think back to when you were getting ready for your show. I doubt there would have been space for me in this room then."

He frowned. "No, not then, but I don't have to drive myself like that anymore, not to that degree." Easy, O'Casey. He mustn't say too much, too soon. God, how he wanted to tell Liberty he loved her, wanted her to marry him, have his baby. But not yet. "The artist and the man don't have to exist in separate worlds." Enough, O'Casey. For Pete's sake, shut up.

"Don't they?" she asked softly. "I think perhaps they do." She stepped back, forcing Finn to drop his hands from her face. She looked at the paintings again, then met his gaze. " 'Art is a jealous mistress.' "

"Ralph Waldo Emerson. But, Liberty, Joseph Story said the same about law, and Robert Louis Stevenson wrote that the open road was his mistress. It can be applied to anything that is important to a man. Or a woman."

"Perhaps," she said, nodding. "But mistresses are demanding as well as jealous, and might refuse to settle for less than total attention."

Finn opened his mouth to reply, then shut it and shook his head. "This conversation is getting nuts. It's all in the abstract. Let's drop it for now and go get something to eat."

"Yes, all right."

At the doorway to the studio, Liberty paused and turned to look at the room once more.

"Thank you for showing me this, Finn. I'll be able to picture you here, creating such beautiful paintings." She looked at him again. "Goodness, I'm hungry. Cleaning dusty bookshelves certainly works up an appetite." She left the room.

Finn turned off the light and followed her, a deep frown on his face. That, he decided, had not gone well. Somehow, everything had gotten off the track. He'd been afraid he'd revealed too much of his feelings at a time when Liberty had enough to deal with. Then, all of a sudden, she was subtly implying that he belonged to his art, and only to his art, that there was no room in his life for anything else. She hadn't seemed particularly upset over the idea, just stated it as fact. Well, it wasn't true, not anymore, but didn't she care if he became a hermit covered in oil paint, loving nothing but his work? Dammit, didn't she care at all? She had to. She just had to.

She did care, he thought fiercely as he followed her down the stairs. She would never have made love with him if she didn't. He knew her do-something-different summers didn't include casual sex. But, Lord above, she was confusing him. Love, as glorious as it was, could very well put him in an early grave!

A strange tension crackled through the air inside Finn's sports car as he drove to the restaurant. Neither he nor Liberty spoke as each concentrated on his own thoughts. But as soft music from the radio drifted around them, and a million stars twinkled in the darkening sky, the tension slowly dissipated, to be replaced by a tingling awareness.

When Finn stopped at a red light, he turned his head to look at Liberty at the exact moment she gazed at him. Their eyes met, and matching smiles touched their lips.

"Hello, Miss Shaw," he said. He reached over and drew his thumb lightly across her lips.

"Hello, Mr. O'Casey," she said. "It's a lovely night. The stars are gorgeous."

"Really beautiful," he said, his gaze never leaving her face.

"Finn?"

"Yes?"

"The light is green."

"Oh," he said, snapping his head back around.

She laughed and he joined her, the happy sound filling the car to overflowing. The mood for the evening was set. Troubles, confusion, and unanswered questions about so many things were pushed to the dusty corners of their minds and not allowed to intrude. The night took on a magical glow of perfection.

"How's your lobster, Liberty?"

"Delicious, absolutely perfect. Is your steak good?"

"Perfect. It's cooked exactly the way I like it." Finn paused. "Did I tell you how pretty you look in that dress?"

"Yes," she said, "but feel free to say it again. I'm beginning to picture myself as Cinderella, as though this night were created for me and my Prince Charming."

"I'll deck the bum. Where is he?"

Liberty's husky laughter flitted through the air, causing heat to throb low in Finn's body.

"You're the Prince, Finn," she said, smiling warmly at him.

"Oh. In that case . . . Just one thing, Cinderella."

"Yes?"

"You can't disappear at midnight." He captured one of her hands. "Got that?"

"Got it." No, she wouldn't disappear that soon, she thought. Nothing, absolutely nothing, was going to spoil this perfect, fairy-tale night. "I won't disappear, Finn."

"Good. There's a band in the other room. Would you like to dance after we've finished eating?"

"Perfect."

So they danced.

Finn held Liberty in his arms, inhaling the light floral fragrance of her hair, feeling her breasts brushing against his chest. Liberty savored Finn's earthy aroma, and the hardness of his body pressed to hers. They swayed to the music, song after song, not noticing when a fast number was played and people bounced, twisted, and whirled around them. They were lost in a world of music only they could hear, oblivious to all and everything else.

When the hour grew late they looked at each other and knew it was time to go. Knew, without saying the words, that Finn would not be taking Liberty back to the apartment over The Book Mark. Knew, as the multitude of silvery stars greeted them when they left the restaurant, that the true magic of the night was yet to come.

In Finn's big bed in his large bedroom, they made love, slow, sweet, sensuous love. They kissed and caressed, holding nothing back, giving and receiving all. Passions flared into a hot flame of want and need, carrying them to heights of fulfillment neither had known before.

"Oh, Finn, Finn."

"Yes, I'm here, right here with you. We'll fly together, Liberty. Now!"

"Yes. Oh, yes!"

They dozed, sated, their heads resting on the same pillow, only to awaken again and reach for each other, beginning once more the journey of ecstasy. Neither wanted the perfect, magical night to end. Neither wished to face all that awaited them in the reality of the light of the new day. The night was theirs.

Jared Loring left the bustling gaming floor of Miracles Casino and walked down a side corridor. He unlocked a door and entered a small office. A few moments later Trig entered, followed closely by the tall, thin Spider.

"Well?" Jared asked. He leaned back against the desk, crossing his arms loosely over his chest. His prematurely silver hair gleamed in the light.

"Nothing, boss," Trig said. "The streets are so quiet, it's enough to give a guy the creeps. My sources don't know a thing, or if they do, they're sure not spilling it."

"Damn," Jared said. "Spider?"

"Ditto. The silence is deafening."

"Don't start talking all highfalutin, Spider," Trig said. "Just admit that you didn't get nothing."

Spider shot Trig a dark glare. "Some of us appreciate the English language, Trigger."

Jared lifted a hand. "Bicker later, gentlemen. I don't like this news. Finn O'Casey is involved in something that I'm beginning to think is bigger than I imagined. The streets don't get this quiet for small potatoes."

" 'Tis true," Spider said, nodding. "I heard Crusher's name once, but then the source clammed up."

"Crusher's in on it," Jared said. "He's Finn's lady's bodyguard."

"Finn's got a lady?" Trig asked. "Hot damn, Tabor is going to like that. She's really into people falling in love with other people. You know what I mean?"

Jared chuckled. "Yes, I know what you mean." He was serious again in the next instant, and ran his hand over the back of his neck. "I really don't like the way this feels. Crusher told Finn to stay out of it and nothing would happen to Finn or Liberty."

"Liberty? Classy name," Trig said. "Don't you think that's a classy name, Spider?"

"Yeah," Spider said thoughtfully. "It has tremendous patriotic overtones."

"Oh, for crying out loud." Trig rolled his eyes

heavenward. "Boss, why can't I work with Marcus? He says one word an hour on a talkative day."

"Could we get back to business here?" Jared asked, raising his eyebrows.

"Oh, sure thing, boss," Trig said. "Did your calls turn up anything?"

"No, nothing. Not a damn thing."

"Strange," Spider said. "Very strange."

"No joke," Trig said. "You have to remember that Finn is Cat O'Casey's kid too. He was right in there pitching during the hoopla with Mickey Mason. I can't see him saluting Crusher and going quietly about his business. Especially if Liberty is in the middle of this. Liberty. I swear, that is one classy, uptown name."

"Trig is right," Spider said. "Finn O'Casey isn't going to sit still long. Wasn't Turtle going to make some calls and see if she could dig up something?"

"Yes," Jared said, "but I'm not very hopeful she did any better than the rest of us. I'll check in with her though." As he reached for the telephone, it rang. He snatched up the receiver. "Loring."

"Oh, Jared," Turtle said. "Oh, just damn it all."

"What's wrong, Turtle?" he asked.

"It's Crusher. Jared, they jumped him, beat him up bad. He's in the hospital in Los Angeles. Crusher and I go way back. We were . . . close many years ago. He's a good man, Jared, and tough. It had to have taken an army to lay him out. I want the scum who did this to him."

"Take it easy, Turtle," Jared said. "Did you find out anything else?"

"No, not a thing. I just got the call about Crusher."

"Okay. Turtle, call the airport and have the pilot get my plane ready. I'm going to L.A."

"Jared, please let me go with you. I have to see Crusher. He's—he's important to me."

"All right. Pack a suitcase and get Sylvia to take over your phones."

"Thanks, honey. Listen, what about Tabor? How are you going to tell her her brother is in a mess again?"

"Very carefully," Jared said, "or she'll be on the next plane from New Orleans. Call Nick and tell him what's going on so he can cover the casino for me. Be ready to leave here in about an hour." He hung up. "Crusher was jumped," he said to Trig and Spider. "Somebody wants a clear path to Liberty Shaw."

"And Finn's the next one standing in the road blocking their way," Trig said. "Who wants Finn's lady, and why?"

Jared pushed himself away from the desk. "That's what I'm going over there to find out. Question is, what do I tell Tabor?"

"Lie," Trig said decisively.

Spider whopped him on the arm. "You don't lie to the woman you love, Trig. It's not socially acceptable behavior. You've been hanging out with the wrong people."

"I've been hanging out with you, idiot," Trig said, glowering at him.

"Well, one would think you would have learned something by now."

"Cork it, gentlemen," Jared said. "Get some sleep, then hit the streets again later. I'll check in with you. Turtle is coming with me. She wants to be with Crusher."

"Turtle and Crusher?" Trig said. "I'll be damned. This love stuff is spreading like a fungus."

"You have absolutely no couth, Trigger," Spider said. "None."

"I'm out of here," Trig said, heading for the door. "Good luck, boss. Talk to you later."

After Trig and Spider had left the office, Jared stared at the telephone for a long moment before shaking his head and lifting the receiver. A few minutes later an obviously sleepy Tabor answered on the other end of the line.

"It's Jared." He could picture her so vividly in his mind, could see her long blond hair in wild disarray, her breasts barely covered by the sheer material of her nightgown. The blood pounded in his veins and his hold on the receiver tightened until his knuckles turned white. "Tabor, I . . ." He cleared his throat roughly. ". . . I have to talk to you."

"In the middle of the night?" she asked, instantly wide awake. "What's wrong?"

"I'll tell you everything, Tabor, but you have to promise me you'll stay in New Orleans and wait to hear from me. You're not to cut your trip short."

"I can't promise that until you've told me what's going on."

"Then I won't tell you. I want your promise."

"That's not fair, Jared Loring."

"That, Tabor Loring, is the way the cards are stacked."

"Darn you, Jared. All right, I'll stay here and finish my business. I promise. Now tell me what's wrong."

"Okay. Here it is. I'm flying to L.A. tonight."

He quickly told Tabor what had taken place.

"My brother is in love and in trouble at the same time? Leave it to Finn. Dear heaven, Jared, what does all this mean?"

"I don't know yet."

"Oh, Jared, Finn is in love for the first time in his life. He'll do anything to protect Liberty, I just know it. And Liberty obviously needs protecting. She's an innocent pawn in—in whatever this is. Thank you for going to them, but please be careful, my darling. That's the promise I want from you."

"You've got it. I'll be in touch as soon as I know something. I love you, Tabor."

"I love you too, Jared. Please call me soon."

"I will. Go back to sleep and dream about me. I miss you like hell, Tabor. 'Bye."

As Jared replaced the receiver, the door opened to admit a tall, dark, handsome man who was fiddling with the tie to his tuxedo.

"I'm here," he said. "Physically. Mentally, I'm still asleep."

"I'm sorry about this, Nick, but I really think I should get over to L.A."

"I agree. Turtle filled me in. Does Tabor know?"

"I just talked to her. She promised to stay in New Orleans and finish the business she went there for."

"Amazing."

"I'm not kidding myself. Tabor will only be able to sit still for a short time. She'll rationalize breaking her promise with some screwy logic that won't make any sense. I've got to pull Liberty and Finn out of this mess before Tabor gets antsy."

"For a *retired* agent you sure seem to do a lot of agent work."

Jared chuckled. "You noticed, huh? Did you also pick up on the fact that it's only since I met Tabor and Finn O'Casey?"

"Tabor is the best thing . . ."

"That ever happened to me," Jared finished for him. "Believe me, I know. I don't want her in the middle of all this." He paused. "It's too quiet on the streets, Nick. Much too quiet."

"Meaning?"

"This is big, whatever it is. Very, very big."

The combined aromas of coffee, soap, and Finn nudged against Liberty's senses and brought her slowly to the surface from her deep cocoon of sleep. She lifted her lashes to find herself looking into Finn's warm brown eyes.

"Good morning," he said, sitting down on the bed. "I come bearing the gift of a mug of coffee."

She smiled and pushed the pillow up behind her, her quick perusal of Finn missing no detail of his muscled physique. He was dressed in jeans and a royal blue dress shirt open at the neck. Insistent tendrils of desire fluttered deep within her. She tucked the sheet over her bare breasts as she leaned against the headboard and accepted the mug.

"Am I being bribed?" she asked after taking a sip of the hot liquid.

"Are you bribable?"

"Probably not, but, then again, it's never come up. This coffee is delicious."

"I hated to wake you, but I figured you'd want to open The Book Mark on time."

"Yes, I do. I'll drink this, then hustle through a shower."

Finn looked at her for a long moment before he spoke again. "Liberty, last night was . . . was very, very special."

"I know," she said, a soft smile on her lips. "Special, beautiful, glorious . . . I could go on and on. A Cinderella night."

"No, that's a fairy tale. What we shared was real."

For now, she thought. Temporarily. She hid the fact that her smile had faded by taking another drink of coffee.

Before Finn could say more, the telephone on the nightstand rang shrilly. Liberty jerked in surprise, nearly spilling her coffee. Finn reached for the receiver.

"Hello?"

"Finn? Jared."

Finn stiffened. "Hi. What's the news?"

"I'm in a hotel here in L.A."

Finn glanced at Liberty, who was watching him intently.

"You're here?" he said. "Why?"

"I'll explain everything when I see you. What are your plans for this morning?"

"Liberty and I are going to The Book Mark to open it."

"Liberty was with you last night? She wasn't in the apartment above the store?"

"She . . . um, yes, she was here last night."

"Who is that?" Liberty whispered. "Who are you telling that I spent the night here?"

Finn flashed her a dazzling smile. "It's 'whom,' and I'm talking to Jared."

"Oh, Lord, how embarrassing."

Jared chuckled. "I heard that. Tell Liberty not to be embarrassed. I'm a big boy, I understand these things." His tone grew serious again. "Finn, I'll meet you at the store. I've rented a car, and I have a map, so I shouldn't have any trouble finding it. Don't go in until I get there."

"Why not? Jared, what is going on?"

"I'll fill you in when we get there. Just don't go inside the store."

"But . . . Jared? Dammit." Finn hung up.

"Jared came over from Las Vegas?" Liberty asked. "Why do I get the feeling he's not making a friendly, family social call?"

Finn got to his feet. "He's meeting us at the store and said not to go inside until he's there."

Her eyes widened. "Why?"

"I don't know. He said he'd explain when he saw us. Hurry, okay? I'll wait for you downstairs." He leaned over and kissed her deeply. "Jared worked as an agent for many years, remember? If he says not to go in the store, then you can be sure there's a good reason for it."

"A frightening reason."

"Not necessarily. He could just be executing extreme caution until he gets a feel for the situation."

"Finn, the man came all the way from Las Vegas, for heaven's sake."

Finn shrugged. "Tabor is in New Orleans on business. Jared might have been restless, glad to have something to do."

Liberty narrowed her eyes. "You're insulting my intelligence."

He sighed. "I'm insulting my own intelligence too. Jared has a casino to run. That he's here is not the best news I've ever had. Well, we won't know any more until we get to the store." He started toward the door. "Get your cute tush in gear, my love."

"Cute tush?" she repeated to the empty room. "I didn't know I had a cute tush. Oh, Liberty, hurry up."

She was showered and floating her gauzy dress over her head in record time, and infinitely grateful the fabric was supposed to have a wrinkled appearance. No one would guess the dress had lain in a heap on the floor all night after Finn had skimmed it from her body.

Jared Loring, she thought, certainly knew where she'd spent the night, but she had no wish to advertise it to the world in general. Her sophistication definitely had its limits.

After seeing the tight set to Finn's jaw as he battled with the morning traffic, Liberty decided not to attempt conversation. A nervous knot twisted in her stomach as they came closer and closer to The Book Mark. Finn miraculously found a parking place two doors away from the store.

"There's Jared," he said, opening his door.

Liberty got out of the car and watched as a tall, well-built man pushed himself away from the building he'd been leaning against. He was dressed in dark slacks, a burgundy-colored shirt, and a light-weight black windbreaker.

Jared Loring, she thought, was extremely handsome. His silver hair was striking, and would turn women's heads wherever he went. There was an intangible aura of authority about him, of strength and power. He obviously could be intimidating, and she was very glad he was on *their* side.

"Fancy meeting you here," Finn said to Jared.

"Hi, Finn."

"Liberty, this is Jared Loring. Jared, Liberty Shaw."

"It's a pleasure, Liberty," Jared said. "It's appropriate that I should meet you under rather bizarre circumstances." He smiled. "After all, you're connected to an O'Casey. They're experts at meeting people under bizarre circumstances."

"Very funny," Finn said dryly. "Isn't it a little warm for a jacket, Jared? Could it be it's hiding a gun?"

Liberty gasped. "A gun?"

"Just jump right in there and scare her to death, Finn," Jared said, shaking his head. "Liberty wasn't raised by Cat O'Casey, remember?" He paused. "Yes, I'm wearing a gun. Crusher was jumped last night. He's in the hospital."

"Oh my God," Liberty said. "Is he going to be all right?"

Jared nodded. "Yes, but he's in rough shape at the moment. Turtle flew over with me, and she's with him."

"Someone wanted Crusher out of the way?" Finn asked. "What in the hell for? To get to Liberty?"

"Me?" she said. "Me?"

"I'm not sure of anything right now," Jared said. "I'm just glad Liberty wasn't here last night. Well, give me the keys and let's check this place out."

Liberty's hands were trembling as she took the keys from her purse and gave them to Jared. Her stomach flip-flopped with fear when Jared pulled a gun from the back of his belt.

"Hang in there, McGee," Finn said, and kissed her on the temple.

"You bet, Fletch." She knew her voice was shaky. "Don't worry about a thing."

"Stay behind me," Jared said, turning the key in the lock. He slowly opened the door, his gun at the ready. "Ah, hell." He stepped inside with Liberty and Finn right behind him.

The color drained from Liberty's face, and she was only vaguely aware of Finn's arm circling her shoulders and pulling her close to his side.

"Dear God," she whispered. "Oh, no, no."

"Damn it to hell," Finn said through clenched teeth. "It's been trashed, totally ransacked. I don't think there's more than a half dozen books left on the shelves."

"It was a thorough job, all right," Jared said, shaking his head as he closed and locked the door. "I'll check the apartment while you wait here."

"The stairs are in the back of the store," Finn said. "Jared, why would anyone—"

"I'll be back in a minute. Liberty? Are you okay?"

"Yes," she said, managing a very weak smile. "Thank you. I'm fine."

Jared crossed the store, stepping over and around the piles of books that had been flung onto the floor.

"This is so frightening, Finn," Liberty whispered.

"I know," he said, tightening his hold on her.

"I'm sorry about this. We'll find out who did it, Liberty, and get all the other answers we don't have. Nothing is going to happen to you, understand? Nothing."

A shiver swept through Liberty as she heard the steely, cold edge to Finn's voice. She nodded, unable to speak.

Jared came back into the store, replacing his gun as he walked toward them.

"The apartment got the same going over," he said.

"Dammit," Finn muttered.

"Oh," was all Liberty could produce.

Jared pushed his jacket back and planted his hands on his hips. "Okay, folks, the first question is very simple."

"Who did this?" Finn said.

"No," Jared said, "not who. That comes later. I need to know—"

"What," Liberty said firmly. "That's the question, right, Jared? *What* were they looking for?"

Seven

"Bingo," Jared said, smiling at Liberty. "What were they looking for?"

"How about that, Spenser?" she said, elbowing Finn in the ribs. "I win the prize."

"You're awesome," he said, and kissed the tip of her nose.

"The prize is that you get to go upstairs and pack your things," Jared said. "Any problem with Liberty staying at your place until we wrap this up, Finn?"

"Fine with me," he said, smiling broadly. "I'll sacrifice myself."

"Let's all go upstairs," Jared said. "We can brainstorm while Liberty is packing."

"What about this awful mess?" she asked.

"Leave it for now," Jared said.

She sighed. "Finn and I had just gotten everything looking so nice. Well, as nice as it was ever going to look. There's just so much a person can do to improve this place."

Upstairs, Liberty hesitated in the doorway when she saw the ransacked disaster of the apartment, then lifted her chin and strode into the bedroom to pack.

"No secrets while I'm in here," she called. "I want to know everything."

Jared chuckled. "Are you sure she doesn't know Tabor, Finn? Why don't you put on a pot of coffee?"

"Okay. Liberty is something, isn't she?"

"I'd say you've chosen well, O'Casey."

"I hear you whispering," Liberty yelled.

Finn and Jared laughed, then Finn went into the kitchen. When Liberty, who had changed into jeans and a yellow-checked blouse, had set her suitcases by the door, she and Finn sat down on the sofa with mugs of coffee. Jared sat in a chair opposite them.

"Where do we start?" Finn asked Jared.

"We don't have all that much," he said. "I think Bev Shaw is alive, and part of a carefully worked out plan put together by the feds. I also think something went wrong, or this place wouldn't have been trashed. The bad guys are after something, and apparently bought the scam that Bev Shaw is dead. If she's dead, she doesn't have whatever it is. So they came looking for it."

"Believe me, Jared," Liberty said, "there's nothing here but books. Finn and I have already searched this place from top to bottom, trying to find a package that a woman named Victoria Manfield was frantic to locate. We certainly didn't come across anything other than a lot of dust."

"Victoria Manfield? A package?" Jared repeated.

"Oh, that has nothing to do with this," Liberty said. "It was a book she was sentimentally attached to that her housekeeper sent down here with other books by mistake. Miss Manfield said Aunt Beverly had wrapped it up and was holding it for her, but Finn and I couldn't find it." She shrugged. "That was the end of that."

Jared leaned forward and rested his elbows on his knees, his coffee mug cradled in his hands. "Manfield."

"Of *the* Manfields," Finn said. "I recognized her from seeing so many pictures of her in the paper. She really pitched a fit when we said we couldn't find the package. I thought she seemed frightened, but Liberty felt she was just upset because she'd lost a keepsake."

"Interesting," Jared said.

"It is?" Liberty asked.

"She said the package contained a book?"

"Yes," Liberty said. "A small book. You know, like a volume of poems, or a diary. I don't know, she didn't say exactly what it was."

"A diary," Finn and Jared said in unison, looking at each other.

"Oh, for Pete's sake, that's silly," Liberty said. "A diary of what? Who Victoria Manfield kissed in the bushes when she was in junior high? I had a fleeting thought that Aunt Beverly had taken it with her when she left here, but I realized that was absurd. One thing I do know for certain is that the package is not in this apartment, or in the store. Maybe Aunt Beverly sent it to Victoria Manfield, and it's lost in the mail."

"Maybe," Jared said.

Liberty looked at Finn, at Jared, then back to Finn. "Why are we spending so much time discussing a package that has nothing to do with anything that is happening now?"

"We have to do things this way sometimes, Liberty," Jared said. "We sort through all the facts to get to the ones we really need, but sometimes we never get a handle on it."

"We have to," Liberty said. "We're going to. My aunt Beverly is alive and out there somewhere. Crusher has been hurt while protecting me. We can't just throw up our hands and say, 'Well, shucks and darn, stick this one in the unsolved stack.' "

Jared smiled at her. "I'm glad you weren't my boss all the years I was an agent." He stood up. "Finn, I checked out of my hotel and thought I'd stay in Tabor's old wing at your house. Let's go back to your place. I have a lot of phone calls to make. I'd guess this fine establishment is now under twenty-four-hour agent surveillance, only they won't be as visible as Crusher was. There's nothing more we can do here for now."

"What do you plan to do first, Jared?" Finn asked.

"Check in with Trig and Spider and see if they've turned up anything interesting. Then I'll have Splice tap into the computer at the Manfield Corporation—I'm assuming they have a computer system—and see just what kind of holdings they're involved in. The Manfield family may have nothing to do with this, but we have so little information we can't afford to leave any stone unturned."

"All right," Finn said, getting to his feet. "Do you have all your things, Liberty?"

"Yes, I—"

The telephone rang.

"Let Liberty answer it," Jared said. "Go ahead, Liberty."

She quickly stood and walked to the end table. Her hand was not quite steady when she lifted the receiver.

"Hello?"

"Liberty, darling, this is your aunt Beverly."

"Aunt Beverly!" she exclaimed. Finn and Jared moved closer to her. "Where are you? So much had happened and . . . Aunt Beverly, please, tell me where you are."

"Oh, Liberty, this was all so carefully worked out, and now everything is going wrong. I never would have involved you if I'd known it would come to this. Since I agreed to be dead, in a manner of speaking, I decided to give you The Book Mark. I did adore that store, but I thought you could sell it and have a tidy nest egg."

"That was very sweet of you, it really was," Liberty said. She held the receiver away from her ear so Finn and Jared could hear what Beverly Shaw was saying. "Are you with federal agents?"

"Yes. They agreed to let me make this one call to urge you to go back to Chicago immediately. I had no intention of putting you in harm's way. Go home, Liberty. Leave the store in the hands of a realtor to sell it for you, and *go back to Chicago.* I'm perfectly safe, doing what I feel I must, and I'm content with my decision. Clarence and Keats are with me, and we're fine."

"Clarence? The attorney?"

"Yes. He's . . . Well, Clarence and I have been, shall we say, fond of each other for many years. He's very sorry that Finn took that tumble over the wastebasket. Clarence had gone back to make certain there were no clues left regarding your meeting in the office. Finn is a dear boy. It would be lovely if you two . . . No, you must go home. Today, Liberty. Get on a plane today."

"Aunt Beverly, I can't do that. I'm involved in this now, whether you meant for that to happen or not."

"No, you mustn't stay."

"Aunt Beverly, does the package you were holding for Victoria Manfield enter into this in any way?"

"I must go. They don't want me to talk any longer. Liberty, I love you. Please, *please*, go home."

"But . . . She hung up," Liberty said, replacing the receiver. "I knew she was alive. I just knew she was. And Keats the cat is with her *and* that sweetie pie Clarence Smith. Jared, why won't the agents tell you what's going on? After all, you were one of them."

"There are a lot of agents, Liberty," Jared said, "and a lot of different kinds. We didn't always see eye-to-eye with each other on how to get the job done, even though we worked for the same government. I'd say that Bev Shaw is with the preppy, suit and tie types. They're not overly fond of those of us who worked undercover. I don't like *them* much either. None of them look old enough to shave, but they're well trained. Stuffy as hell, but well trained. Your aunt is safe, you can be sure."

"What if they decide that Liberty needs tighter protection?" Finn asked.

"You mean whisk me off somewhere?" Liberty said. "Not on your life, bub. I'm not getting stuffed in a room to play solitaire until this is over."

"They want you to go back to Chicago," Jared said.

She crossed her arms over her breasts. "No, I won't go. I came here for the summer, and I'm staying."

Only for the summer? Finn repressed the question and it's implications. They had to get on with the matter at hand.

"My lady has spoken," he said, smiling.

"I certainly have," Liberty said decisively. She paused. "Do you think it was a coincidence that Aunt Beverly was told to hang up as soon as I asked about Victoria Manfield's package?"

Finn shrugged. "Beats me."

"I'm not sure either," Jared said. "Maybe we'll know more once Splice gathers the info on the Manfields. Let's hit the road."

"Well, Fletch," Liberty said, smiling at Finn, "at least we solved the mystery of the missing cat food."

"You betcha, McGee. We're a terrific team." A team, he thought. A twosome. A couple. Oh, how he loved this woman.

A team, Liberty mused, as they crossed the room. Liberty and Finn. Together. Loving and in love. How glorious it would be. But daydreams like that were the stuff of which fairy tales were made. And this, darn it, was cold, harsh reality. Art was still a jealous mistress. Art had staked a claim on

Finn's heart and would hold fast. Art would always be his first love.

Back in the huge, sprawling house in Beverly Hills, Jared disappeared into Tabor's wing after telling Finn and Liberty he would meet them in Finn's kitchen at noon to report in and have some lunch.

"A person could get lost in here for days," Liberty said, glancing around. "It's even bigger than I thought it was last night."

Finn chuckled. "It is a bit large. Sometimes I think I should speak with Tabor about selling it. Then I remember the good times we had here, and postpone bringing it up. Plus, my studio was made to my exact specifications. I could have it duplicated somewhere else, I suppose. I'll talk it over with Tabor one of these days."

"I can understand your not wanting to sell a home that has happy memories of your childhood, Finn. I never lived in one place long enough to fill a thimble with memories."

"Until Chicago," he said quietly.

"Yes," she said, meeting his gaze, "until Chicago."

Damn, Finn thought. "Well," he said, forcing a lightness into his voice, "California hasn't proved to be exactly dull for you. It's not everyone who gets caught up in the middle of a mystery."

She smiled. "That's true. I'm not sure the Chamber of Commerce would approve." And not everyone who came to California fell in love either. But she had. Oh, yes, she had. "Finn," she went on in a more serious tone, "do you honestly think we'll find out what's going on with Aunt Beverly?"

"If anyone can piece it together, Jared can. Let's go to my wing and relax. And, Liberty, don't go outside of the house unless you're with me or Jared. I'm not trying to scare you, but it doesn't hurt to be cautious. I'm very grateful you weren't alone in that apartment above The Book Mark last night."

She laughed. "Even the bad guys know I didn't sleep in my own bed."

"Will your parents be calling to check on you?"

"No. I phoned when I arrived, and we'll just go back to weekly letters now. My father is furious that Aunt Beverly left me the store. She is, quote, 'Corrupting me with her black sheep ways from the grave, dragging me into a sordid and seedy part of town.' He really said sordid and seedy. Little does he know that Aunt Beverly is alive, and snug as a bug with her lover and her cat. Of course, he doesn't know his daughter is with her lover too. Poor man. He'd freak out. I think I'll always be a child in his eyes."

"In *my* eyes," Finn said, circling her shoulders with his arm, "you are most definitely a woman." His woman.

And he was a man, she thought. Her man. For now. "Why, thank you, sir. I guess I should hang up some of my clothes before they're a wrinkled mess. I certainly seem to do a lot of packing and unpacking these days."

How would she feel about packing for a honeymoon trip? Finn wondered as they walked down the hall. Well, one thing was for sure. When Finn

O'Casey fell in love, he didn't mess around. He really went for it all—wife, kids, dog, cat, PTA meetings. Damn, it sounded good. He and Liberty would fill their home with so much love, laughter, and warmth, there would never be room for the slightest chill of loneliness for anyone.

But it would never happen if Liberty didn't love him.

"Liberty," he said as they entered his living room. She turned to face him. "Yes?"

"I . . . Nothing. Go ahead and unpack in my room."

"Well, not everything. After all, this whole business about Aunt Beverly could be cleared up in a flash, and I would be going back to the apartment."

"Oh? You will?"

"Yes, of course. I mean, I can't move in here for the remainder of the summer." Or the remainder of her life.

Finn lightly cupped her neck with his hands. He traced the line of her jaw with his thumbs as he looked directly into her eyes.

"Why not?" he asked quietly. "Why can't you stay here with me?"

The sensual stroking of Finn's thumbs made Liberty shiver. "I'm—I'm moving in here now, Finn, because of what happened at The Book Mark. It's a little late for me to be insisting on sleeping in one of the guest rooms and, well, I wouldn't want to. But to stay on after this trouble is over . . . Finn, I've never lived with a man before. I'm rationalizing my being here now by telling myself it isn't safe in the apartment. But later when . . .

Oh, wonderful, I sound so childish, so foolish. I'm not making any sense."

"Yes, you are," he said, smiling at her. "You're saying you're not taking our being together lightly, and I cherish that. Liberty, I've never lived with a woman either. There hasn't been anyone important enough to me . . . anyone I wanted to make love with at night, wake up next to in the morning, spend the day together, then make love with again. No one, until you."

She stepped back, forcing him to drop his hands from her throat. Her eyes filled with unexpected tears.

"We're not permanent, Finn, remember? We're all caught up in this mess about Aunt Beverly. It'll be solved somehow, and then . . . Then the rest of the summer passes, do-something-different time is over, and that's that."

"Liberty—"

"It's temporary, what we have," she went on, tears spilling onto her cheeks. "Your mistress, your art, will call your name and you'll go to her, devote yourself to her, which is the way it should be. You have to do that, and I understand because you have such a beautiful and rare gift."

"But, I—"

"And I'll go back to Chicago and teach school. Chicago. Where I belong. I hate it, but it's mine and—Oh, God, so much is happening so quickly." She dashed the tears from her cheeks. "Some of it is a nightmare, and some is like a glorious dream, and it's all mixing up together, and I hardly know what's real or what isn't, and . . ."

"Liberty."

He pulled her close, one arm circling her back, his other hand weaving through her auburn hair and pressing her head on his chest.

Damn your hide, O'Casey, he fumed at himself. He'd pushed her, rushed her, knowing she had too much to handle now. The situation with Bev wasn't remotely close to what people went through in their everyday lives, and Liberty had been tossed right into the middle of it. She'd been so damn brave, hanging in there every step of the way.

Her quiet crying tore at his heart, and he tightened his hold on her, wanting to comfort her, yet not knowing what to say.

He'd blown it, he raged at himself. He could win the Olympic gold medal for his stupidity.

She slowly lifted her head. "I'm sorry," she said, not meeting his gaze. "Everything just caught up with me, I guess."

"You have every right to cry," he said gently. "Look, why don't you hang up your clothes, then stretch out on the bed? I'll come get you when Jared shows up for lunch. Okay?"

"Yes," she said, nodding. "That sounds like a good idea."

"Could you look at me for a minute?"

"I'm an icky crier. My nose gets red and my eyes get puffy."

"I'll survive the shock. Look at me."

She slowly met his gaze, and his heart thudded painfully when he saw tears still shimmering in her big brown eyes.

She appeared so small and vulnerable, he thought. He wanted to hold her close and protect her, never again let her go. It was his fault her eyes were puffy and her nose was red, his fault she'd cried. Well, from here on out, he was going to keep his big mouth shut, take this one step at a time the way it should be done.

He brushed his lips over hers. "Go rest. You're all worn out. Liberty, everything is going to be all right, you'll see."

She nodded, attempted a smile that failed, then moved out of his arms and left the room.

Finn watched her go, resisting the urge to follow her, to tell her he'd hold her while she slept. He pulled his gaze from the doorway she'd disappeared through and glanced around the large living room.

A chill swept through him as he stood alone in the huge, empty room.

"Jared Loring. Now, why aren't I surprised to hear your voice after all these years?"

Jared cradled the phone between his ear and shoulder, and propped his feet on the coffee table.

"Oh, I'd say because you don't miss much that goes on, chief," Jared said. "You've heard, I'm sure, that I've got people on the streets trying to dig up info on this Bev Shaw thing. And, being the wise and wonderful master of the troops you are, I'm quite positive you know that Finn O'Casey is involved in this. Finn being, of course, my brother-in-law, and Cat's son."

"Wise and wonderful master? You should have shown me such respect when you worked for me, you rebel. Flattery, Loring, is going to get you zip."

"Hank, lighten up. You've got a deal cooking that is going bad really fast. I'm sure it looked great on paper, but it's being blown apart. The fact that Crusher is in the hospital is evidence of that. You lucked out when Liberty Shaw wasn't in that apartment last night. You've got a private citizen smack-dab in the middle of this."

Hank sighed. "I know. It should have gone like clockwork but . . . Well, these things happen."

"Liberty Shaw got the call from Bev, but Liberty isn't budging."

"Dammit, Jared, get that girl on a plane headed for Chicago. Today."

"I know zip, remember? Actually, I'm a private citizen, too, and so is Finn."

"Bull. Try telling Mickey Mason that. Lord, that was a sweet deal you pulled on the Mouse. I've waited years to nail that sleaze."

"So, you owe Finn and me one each, and we're calling in our debt. Would you like me to tell you what I know so far about this fiasco?"

"No," Hank said, chuckling. "You'll drive my blood pressure up. I imagine you've pieced it together very well."

"There are some holes that need plugging, but I think I'm getting the drift. Try the name Manfield on for size."

"Damn you, Loring, you're going to give me another ulcer."

Jared laughed. "I'll ship you a case of antacids. Okay," he went on, serious again. "Bev Shaw is in a safe house under wraps. She was ready to retire to the sand and surf with the love of her life, cute Clarence. So, you struck a deal. She plays dead, you buy her store, Liberty inherits it. In exchange, you get Victoria Manfield's diary. Bev is in no danger and can quietly disappear later. After all, she's dead, right? Liberty is in no danger because she just arrived on the scene, knowing nothing. Being the ever-cautious chief that you are, Crusher came in as added insurance. But surprise . . . the nasty types didn't follow the script."

"Are you finished yet, smart mouth?" Hank asked gruffly.

"Not quite. Lord, Hank, didn't you think they'd come looking for the diary?"

"No. Victoria Manfield had Liberty search for it, Liberty couldn't find it, Victoria accepted that. Not happily, but she did accept it. Bev Shaw is a scatterbrain, and Victoria knew it, knew Bev could have stashed the thing heaven only knows where. Victoria, according to my man on the inside, was ready to cut and run. It's her father who's causing the screwup."

"What's in the diary?" Jared asked.

"Bank account numbers and the phony names on each one. Plus, a record of who paid Manfield what amount for favors rendered."

"Such as?"

"Construction jobs worth millions that were supposed to be awarded after submission of sealed bids. Money changed hands, the bids were ignored. Payola, chum. Then there's the city council member that Manfield has in his hip pocket. Manfield acts as middleman. Someone wants some land zoned to his advantage, and Manfield pays the councilman after taking a nice percentage for himself off the top."

"Interesting," Jared said. "Manfield is a busy boy."

"The whole family is in on it. Mama Manfield got some drug charges against a friend's kid dropped . . . for a price. Baby brother specializes in illegal aliens. Victoria darling flits around with her fingers in a lot of pies. The list is long."

"I knew it was big. So? What's the holdup here?"

"We want to nab everyone who's involved, and we have to be careful, coordinate it down to the last detail. There are so many people in high places that are going to take a fall on this, and we don't want anyone slipping through the net. We've just gotten the arrest warrants we need, and now we're planning the move. You wouldn't believe how many men I have on this."

"Time is your enemy, Hank. You're running the risk of a leak."

"I realize that, but if we go in sloppy we'll lose some of them. My man says Manfield is keeping it quiet. The old boy is convinced he can find the diary and go back to business as usual. I can't make my move yet, Jared, I'm not ready. In the meantime, Liberty Shaw is in danger. I never intended for her to be in any jeopardy at all. Well, there you have it. You're right, it's big. Wait until the thing goes down. You'll be shocked when you find out who's as crooked as the day is long. This town is going to come unglued."

"Hank, Manfield has got to be shaking in his shorts. He's already using muscle instead of money to find that book."

"I know. That's why I want Liberty Shaw on the next plane to Chicago. I'm sure word is on the streets that you're in town, but I'm hoping they'll chalk it up to your paying a visit to your brother-in-law. Leave it to Finn to fall for Liberty and muddy the waters. My life is never simple."

"When are you going to make your move, Hank?"

"I'm working as fast I can. Hopefully, we'll go in a couple of days. This thing is so damn big, and I've got so many agents out there, I feel like Patton trying to coordinate a war. They all have to pounce at once. Ten minutes difference could mean we lose some of the scum. I don't intend to lose any of them."

"I get the picture. Look, Finn and I will take care of Liberty. You can cross protecting her off your list of things to do."

"I appreciate that, Jared. I'll call you and keep you up-to-date. I swear, when this one is over, I'm going on a long vacation. Well, stick close to Liberty Shaw, Jared. It's good to have you aboard. I don't suppose you'd consider . . ."

"Coming back? Not a chance. I have a wonderful wife, a new house we're considering filling up with little Lorings, and a casino that's making me a very wealthy man. Can you top that?"

"Nope. I can envy you it all though. I've got to go. I'll be in touch. In the meantime, you and O'Casey take very good care of Liberty Shaw."

"Count on it. Good luck, Hank."

"I'm going to need it."

Jared replaced the receiver, then laced his hands behind his head. "I knew it was big," he said to no one. "Hell, it's gigantic." And he'd better fill Finn and Liberty in pronto.

He stood and started across the room, only to

be stopped by the shrill ringing of the telephone. He spun around and snatched up the receiver halfway through the second ring.

"Loring."

"Jared Loring?"

"Yes."

"I was given this number by someone at your Miracles Casino in Las Vegas. I've been trying very hard to reach you. This is Captain Bardot of the New Orleans Police Department."

Every muscle in Jared's body instantly tightened. "Yes?"

"I'm sorry to have to tell you this, but Mrs. Loring has been in an automobile accident."

No! Jared felt like screaming. "And?" he asked, unaware that he was hardly breathing.

"She's going to be fine, Mr. Loring. Let me assure you of that."

"Thank God," Jared whispered, running a shaking hand down his face. "Oh, Tabor."

"Mr. Loring?"

"Yes, yes, I'm here. What—what are the extent of Tabor's . . . Mrs. Loring's injuries?"

"She has a broken right foot, a mild concussion, and a great many bruises. She's asking for you, Mr. Loring, and I promised her I would contact you myself."

"You said someone at the casino gave you this number? Tabor knew I had come here to L. A."

"Oh? Well, the concussion, you know. She's a bit fuzzy. May I assume that I can assure her you're on your way?"

"Yes, of course. What hospital is she in?"

"I'll have a police car waiting for you at the

airport. We have access to the airline computers, and we'll know which flight you were able to get. Please don't worry, Mr. Loring, your wife is going to be fine. She simply needs your comforting presence. I'll go tell her now that I've spoken with you."

"You're very kind. What hospital did you—Damn," he muttered when he heard the dial tone humming in his ear.

He slammed down the receiver and ran from the room to find Finn. He had to tell him what had happened in New Orleans, bring him up-to-date on what he'd learned about the Bev Shaw situation, impress upon him the necessity to carefully protect Liberty, and then get to Tabor.

Get to Tabor!

Get to Tabor!

Get to Tabor. . . .

Eight

A loud, heavy boom of thunder woke Liberty from a deep sleep. She sat bolt upright on the bed, having absolutely no idea where she was. The room was in semidarkness, rain beat against the windows, and she blinked several times, trying to clear her foggy mind. The clock on the nightstand next to the king-size bed said it was nearly four o'clock.

Finn's bed, she thought. Finn's house. Finn's clock. Yes, she remembered now. Finn was to have awakened her for lunch. She'd nearly slept the day away. He must have decided she needed the rest more than food. And judging by her earlier weepy performance, he was probably right.

She slid off the bed and went into the bathroom to splash water on her face and run a brush through her hair. After putting on her shoes, she went in search of Finn and Jared.

Finn was sitting on the sofa in the living room

reading a newspaper by the light of a lamp on the end table. He'd had to turn the lamp on because the raging storm had made the day dark as night. He looked up as she entered the room.

"Well, you had quite a nap," he said. He folded the paper and put it on the coffee table. "Feeling better?"

"Much better, thank you. I thought you were going to wake me."

He patted the cushion next to him and she sat down.

"You were sleeping so peacefully," he said, "that I hated to disturb you. I know you missed lunch, but you can have a big dinner." His gaze slid over her features, one by one. "Hello, Liberty Shaw."

"Hello, Finn O'Casey."

He kissed her deeply, his tongue delving into her mouth to explore each hidden crevice. His hands roamed restlessly over her back, then moved to her breasts. Liberty leaned into the kiss, and into Finn, seeking more, savoring all.

He lifted his head. "We have to talk before you make me forget what I'm supposed to tell you."

"Oh, yes, certainly. What are we talking about?"

"In a minute," he said, and took possession of her mouth once more.

Desire throbbed insistently within Liberty as she fervently returned the kiss. The kiss became frenzied, and they both gasped for breath. The rain beat against the windows, thunder rumbled, lightning crackled like a sharp whip, but neither Liberty nor Finn noticed or cared.

At last, Finn jerked his head up. "No more," he said, his voice raspy. "You are one potent lady, my lady. Oh, Lord, how I want you. Right now."

She ran a fingertip over his lips. "I want you too. Couldn't we talk later?"

"You bet." He paused. "No! What I mean is, it's important that I bring you up-to-date on what has happened, what Jared found out."

She sighed. "All right." She glanced up at the ceiling. "That certainly is a noisy storm."

"Summer storms are like that here. They move in fast too. I like the rain, the thunder and the lightning. To me it's nature's way of saying slow down, folks, remember the basics—rain, sunshine, air to breathe. You know, the old philosophy of taking time to smell the flowers."

" 'Love comforteth like sunshine after rain,' " she said. "Where's Jared?"

"Shakespeare," Finn said, "and Jared had to go to New Orleans. Tabor's been in an automobile accident."

"What? Is she all right?"

"She's going to be fine. She has a slight concussion and a broken foot. She wanted Jared with her."

"My goodness, yes, I would certainly think so. Oh, Finn, I'm so sorry. Jared must have been terribly upset. You must be worried too. Heavens, you could have gone with him if you weren't stuck here babysitting me."

"Hey, enough of that kind of talk. In the first place, being with you is where I want to be, where I belong." Just like Jared belonged with Tabor, he thought, because that was part of being in love. "And in the second place, Tabor asked for Jared, not me, which is the way it should be. He'll call later after he's seen her and tell us how she is."

"He didn't speak with her on the phone?"

"No, the police called him. Before he left, he brought me up-to-date on what he'd found out about your aunt Bev. In fact, he had the entire story."

"You're kidding. Well, we got a few pieces of the puzzle, Fletch. That's not so shabby for a couple of amateurs."

"Indeed not, McGee. We did ourselves proud." He gave her a fast, hard kiss. "Okay, here's the scoop . . ."

Liberty listened intently as Finn told her all that Jared had learned. ". . . and there you have it," he finished.

"Unbelievable," she said, shaking her head. "There are so many people involved in this. Finn, shouldn't Aunt Beverly have simply turned over the diary to the agents like a good citizen once she realized what it contained? I mean, it sounds as though she held out for money or something."

"I asked Jared about that. Bev was given, in essence, a reward for finding something that was extremely valuable to her country. There were various options open to the agents. In all honesty, Liberty, your aunt is not a candidate for the witness protection program. She's a talker, a people collector. She'd spill the beans for sure. She's in the safe house now and is believed to be dead. Considering her personality, this is the best road to go. I know where your mind is headed, but The Book Mark is officially and legally yours with your government's blessings."

She nodded. "I see."

"Now, here's the heavy part. This operation is

so big, Jared told his old boss not to spare men to protect you, that he and I would take care of you. Jared had to leave, so it's just you and me, kid. We're not budging from this house, Liberty. It should only be a couple of days. There's plenty of food, we'll be fine."

"They still think I'm in danger?"

"Manfield is a desperate man. He can't accept defeat without a fight. He's determined to find that diary, and he seems to be convinced you know where it is. I guess it hasn't occurred to him that the feds might have it. He has to find it or he and a bunch or other big shots, including the whole Manfield family, are headed for the slammer."

"The slammer?" Liberty repeated with a burst of laughter. "I don't think detectives say 'slammer' anymore."

"Up the river? The big house? Oh, well, forget it. The point is, this is almost over, but not quite, and until it is, we stay put."

"Just the two of us?" she asked, batting her eyes. "Alone?"

"It's a nasty assignment I've been given here," he said with a dramatic sigh, "but someone has to do it."

She punched him on the arm. He laughed and stood, grabbing her hand and hauling her up too.

"Come along, my love, and I'll feed you," he said. "The protector must not allow the protectee to fade away to a mere shadow of her former self. There are rules about this stuff, you know."

"Do tell."

"Yep. By the way, I turned on the security system so don't open any doors or windows, or you'll set it off. We're snug as bugs here, my dear."

"Thank you, Finn," she said, smiling at him.

He drew one thumb over her cheek. "The pleasure is all mine."

"I hope Jared calls soon with a report on Tabor. I'm sure you're worried about your sister, and I feel as though I know her."

"He'll call as soon as he can. Let's eat."

It seemed like an eternity to Jared before the plane touched down in New Orleans. He was convinced the pilot had landed at every airport between Los Angeles and New Orleans like a bus driver seeing if anyone happened to want a ride.

Jared grabbed his small carry-on bag and inched his way down the aisle of the plane, relieved that at least he wasn't facing the hassle of baggage claim. His muscles ached from tension, for he'd been unable to relax during the flight. His thoughts had centered on Tabor and his driving need to be with her.

Yet, he knew there had been more eating at him, keeping him in turmoil. His little voice, which had held him in good stead during his years as an agent, had nagged at him, refused to leave him alone during the seemingly endless flight.

Something wasn't right.

Something just wasn't right.

Jared emerged from the jetway and strode across the busy airport, weaving his way around the people in his path. As he went out the door, he was hit by heavy, humid, hot air. Night had fallen, and amber lights cast an eerie glow in the parking lot beyond the terminal.

A police car was parked at the curb directly in front of him. Glancing around, he saw a young officer slipping a ticket under the windshield wiper of the vehicle in front of the patrol car. Jared stepped off of the curb as the officer returned to his car.

"Excuse me," Jared said. "Are you looking for Jared Loring?"

"Not that I know of. Is he wanted for something?"

"No, I'm Jared Loring, and Captain Bardot said a patrol car would be waiting to give me a ride to the hospital."

"Captain who?" the policeman asked.

"Bardot."

The officer shook his head. "Never heard of him, but I haven't been on the force very long. Tell you what. Get in the passenger side there, and I'll radio into central dispatch and find out what precinct Bardot is in. Could be that your pickup car had to respond to a call on the way here."

"Thanks. I really appreciate your help."

"No problem."

The knot in Jared's stomach coiled tighter and his little voice started shouting. He narrowed his eyes and got into the patrol car. As the officer reached for the radio, Jared suddenly knew without a glimmer of a doubt that there was no Captain Bardot in the New Orleans Police Department.

Fury burned within him like hot lava, and a rushing noise roared in his ears.

"Mr. Loring?"

"What?" Jared said, snapping his head around.

"There's no Captain Bardot on the force. Are you sure you got the name right?"

"Very sure," Jared said. He opened the car door. "Thanks."

"Someone played a joke on you, huh?"

"Something like that." He got out and closed the door.

The officer shrugged, started the car, and pulled away from the curb. Jared ran down the sidewalk to a telephone booth. He shoveled some coins into the box, dialed a number, and a few minutes later a very familiar voice came on the line.

"Hello?"

"Hello, Tabor."

"Jared, how nice. I was just thinking about you, and missing you like crazy. So? What's going on there at Finn's?"

"Tabor, I'm here in New Orleans."

"Here? Why?"

"Listen, I'll be right over to your hotel. Stay in your room, and don't open the door unless you're sure it's me."

"All right, but what is—"

"I'll explain when I see you. Your hotshot ex-agent of a husband has been conned, Tabor. I've got to call Finn, then I'll grab a taxi and come to your hotel. Stay put. I love you."

Jared broke the connection, pushed in another coin, and dialed '0'.

"Operator."

"Credit card call," Jared said.

"Go ahead, sir."

Jared recited his credit card number, then Finn's phone number, and waited, tapping his fingers impatiently.

"I'm sorry, sir, that number is temporarily out of order. I'm unable to complete your call."

"Thank you," he said, and slowly replaced the receiver. "Damn you, Manfield," he said under his breath. "Damn you straight to hell."

He left the booth and ran to the taxi stand. Two twenty-dollar bills flashed under the driver's nose got Jared the guarantee that no time would be wasted in reaching Tabor's hotel.

"Finn," Liberty said, "if you keep glowering at the phone like that, you're going to melt it."

Finn drummed his fingers on the top of the receiver. "I just wish Jared would . . ." He snatched up the phone. "Ring, you dolt. I need to know—Ah, hell!"

"What's wrong?"

"It's dead. The phone is dead. The lines must be down from this storm." He slammed the receiver back into place and lunged to his feet. "Terrific. Just great. Jared can't get through with a report on Tabor. I know she's all right, but I want to hear him say the words." He began to pace the floor. "The phones could be out for hours. You never know when one of these storms goes nuts like this one."

"Finn, couldn't we go to a phone booth? We could just keep driving around until we found one that's working. All the lines can't be down."

He stopped in his trek and looked at her. "We're not leaving this house, Liberty."

"But . . ."

"Besides, Jared didn't say what hospital Tabor was in. I'm not even sure he knew because a policeman was going to pick him up at the airport."

"Then we'll call the New Orleans police."

"Dammit, Liberty," he yelled, "I said we're not leaving the house."

She threw up her hands. "I don't know what else to suggest. I feel terrible that you're so upset about Tabor and you're stuck in here because of me. I think we'd be safe enough if we stayed together out there. I hate seeing you like this."

He sat down beside her and slid one arm across her shoulders. "Hey," he said gently, "I'm sorry. I shouldn't have taken it out on you. It was just so frustrating to realize I've been sitting here for hours waiting for that phone to ring, and the dumb thing wasn't even working. I apologize for yelling at you."

"You're forgiven. But I still think we could go out together and—"

"No. We're not running any risks. Jared is taking care of Tabor, and I'm taking care of you, and that's the way it is. I'll just have to be patient and wait until Jared can get through to me to report on Tabor. Want some popcorn?"

"Popcorn? You certainly change subjects fast."

"It's"—he glanced at his watch—"nearly ten. I'll make some popcorn, then we'll be all set to watch the late movie. Deal?"

"Buttered popcorn?"

"Yep."

"Deal."

"What else can I talk you into?" he asked, lowering his head toward hers.

"Something to drink?"

He slid his tongue along her bottom lip. "I might be persuaded to include drinks with my offer." He kissed one side of her mouth, then the other. "What do you want?"

A shiver of desire swept through her as Finn outlined her lips with the tip of his tongue. "What do I want what . . . when . . . I mean . . . Finn, you're driving me crazy."

"I'm investigating, McGee," he said, planting nibbling kisses down the side of her neck. "Mmm, just as I thought. You taste better than buttered popcorn."

Her attempt to laugh came out as a gasp as he found the pulse point at the base of her throat. Her heart beat wildly and her breasts grew heavy, aching for Finn's soothing touch.

"Finn . . . " she whispered.

His mouth claimed hers in a hot, searing kiss. She nearly sobbed with relief as she parted her lips to meet his tongue with her own. He gathered her close, crushing her sensitive breasts to his chest in a sweet pain. She sank her fingers into his hair, loving its silky texture, the way it fell naturally back into place, loving Finn.

"Liberty," Finn murmured, "I"—*love you*—"want you." Will always love you. And soon, very soon, he'd be able to tell her.

"I want you too, Finn," she said. And she loved him with every breath in her body.

"Popcorn."

"Tomorrow. We'll have popcorn for breakfast."

"Good idea. You're sure smart, Ms. Marple."

"I know, Poirot. Maybe we should move this discussion into the bedroom and—"

The lights went out, and the room was instantly an inky well of darkness.

"Dammit." Finn said. "That caps it. I'm moving to Alaska."

"Good grief, it's dark in here," Liberty said, clinging to his shoulders. "Does this happen a lot too? Like the phones going kaput?"

"Yep. These storms are oodles of fun."

"You said that you liked them."

"I did, but this one's timing is not high on my list. Sit tight. My eyes have adjusted enough to the darkness so I can move around. Listen, don't get shook up when I say this, but I'm going into my bedroom and get my gun."

"I'm shook up. Why do you want your gun?"

"I'd just feel better if I had it with me. The security system goes off when the electricity does. Don't budge."

"I won't because I can't see a thing."

"I'll be right back."

" 'Kay."

She felt Finn move away, then blinked several times, straining her eyes as she looked into the darkness around her. Shapes slowly took form. A chair, a lamp, an end table. Nothing was totally clear, but at least she didn't feel as though she'd fallen into a black tunnel. They'd light some candles and . . . Say now, candles were really very romantic. The storm wasn't all bad.

Suddenly she heard the sound of breaking glass from far down the hall. She jumped to her feet, staring in the direction the noise had come from. Trembling fingers pressed to her lips, she listened intently, hoping to hear Finn coming back down the hall.

Silence.

There was only silence that seemed as heavy as the darkness pressing in around her, making it difficult to breathe.

Where was Finn? she wondered frantically. What glass had broken with that sickening sound? Why hadn't Finn come back? Or called out to her that he was fine and had just broken something? Oh, God, why was it so unearthly quiet in there, so very dark? Where was Finn?

Calm down, Liberty Shaw, she told herself, dropping her fingers from her lips. There was a reasonable explanation for this. Yes, of course, there was. Finn would pop into the room any second now and tell her what had broken, and why he'd been gone so long. So, where in the blue blazes was he? Oh, Lord, what if he was hurt? What if whatever had broken had broken all over Finn? It had definitely been glass. He could be bleeding and—Calm down!

Liberty pressed her hand to her heart, then took a deep breath and let it out slowly. She was going down that dark cave of a hallway, she decided. She was going to find Finn. And if she discovered he was fine, was simply taking his own sweet time coming back to the living room, she'd sock him in the eye!

She bent over slightly and held one hand out in front of her as she made her way forward. The furniture was still nothing more than various shadowy shapes. End table. Check. Telephone on end table. Check. Lamp. Check. She had a clear path now, between there and the hall. Clear as mud, and with her luck she'd probably smack right into the wall.

One step forward. Another. Then another, both of her arms now straight out in front of her, her heart beating a rapid tattoo.

And then she heard it. The cough.

It came from somewhere down the hall. It had been muffled, but she'd heard it.

And she knew, she definitely knew, that it had not been Finn who had coughed.

There was someone in the house!

Chilling fear swept through her, then in the next instant she was hot and clammy, swaying slightly on her feet. She could taste the fear in her mouth. Paralyzing fear.

Finn! she screamed silently.

She squeezed her eyes tightly closed for a moment, forcing herself under control, telling herself that Finn wasn't coming, that someone else was in that hall. Telling herself that she was alone.

She opened her eyes and turned, carefully retracing her steps. She moved to the far end of the sofa, brushing her fingertips across the end table. They met a large, heavy glass ashtray. She picked it up and crept onto a high-backed leather chair. She sank to her knees behind the chair, clutching the ashtray to her breasts as though it were a precious treasure.

She waited, and listened.

A sob caught in her throat as the beam of a flashlight snaked over the room.

"Don't be tiresome, Miss Shaw," a deep voice said. "We don't have time for childish games. Bo, check the kitchen."

Dear heaven, Liberty thought, there were two of them, if not more. What had they done to her beloved Finn? How badly had they hurt him? No, she mustn't think about that now.

"Nobody in the kitchen, Mr. Manfield," a rumbly voice said.

Manfield? Liberty thought. Oh, that despicable, rotten man.

"She's in here somewhere," Manfield said.

"You shouldn't have had me dump the fuses. If I had 'em, I could get us some light in here."

"I'll find her soon enough. Miss Shaw? Why not save us both a lot of trouble? Your lover is of no use to you. I have no wish to harm you, I simply want the book. Give it to me and I'll be on my way. I'll even stop and report your electrical and phone problems. Fair enough? Come, come, Miss Shaw, we're wasting time. Let's complete our business, shall we?"

Over my dead body, Liberty thought fiercely. Oh, mercy, what a terrible choice of words.

The flashlight beam continued to sweep the room in a steady pattern. Liberty set the ashtray on the carpet, slipped off one of her shoes, and waited. When the light was on the opposite side of the room, she stood and hurled the shoe as hard as she could, ducking back down in the next instant.

"Ow! Dammit, she busted my nose! God, I'm in pain."

"Shut up, Bo," Manfield said.

"You'd yell, too, if you were bleeding to death," Bo said. "Oh, my nose, my nose."

Lucky shot, Liberty thought. She sure couldn't hit anything when she played the games at carnivals. So, now what? She was buying some time, but what good was it going to do her? Oh, God, she was so scared.

"I'm getting some ice for this nose," Bo said.

"Dammit, Bo, I want you to help me find her."

"In a minute. Keep your shirt on."

When Manfield spoke again, Liberty's eyes widened. He was coming across the room, she realized. Closer and closer . . .

"Miss Shaw?" he said. "I've had quite enough of this nonsense."

Closer and closer . . .

She grabbed the ashtray with both hands.

Closer . . .

She jumped to her feet. "Fletch!" she yelled. "McGee! Um . . . Donder and Blitzen! Move in!"

Manfield spun around to shine the flashlight down the hall. Liberty flung the ashtray at his head with all she was worth, and heard a resounding thud.

"Oh, Lord," she whispered, as he crumbled into a heap on the floor. "I've killed him."

Her head snapped up when she heard the sound of pounding feet and the back door being thrown open.

" 'Bye, Bo," she said, with an hysterical little giggle.

In the next moment the front door exploded into flying splinters of wood, and two men rolled into the room. She screamed at the top of her lungs.

"Liberty Shaw!" one of the men yelled.

She kept right on screaming.

"Liberty!"

And screaming.

"Jared sent us!"

She stopped in mid-scream. "Oh," she said,

"that's nice." She blinked. "Oh my God, Finn. We've got to find Finn. Please, please, help me find Finn."

"I'm here, McGee," a weak voice said.

The two men got to their feet and switched on flashlights. Finn was leaning against the far wall, one hand on his head.

"Finn!" Liberty exclaimed, and ran across the room to him. He caught her tightly with his free arm. "Are you all right?"

"Oh, Liberty, I'm so damn sorry. They came through that window and had me before I knew what happened. Some protector I am." He tightened his hold on her even more. "Are you hurt? I'm so sorry."

"I'm fine, but, Finn, I killed Mr. Manfield. I broke Bo's nose and then . . . Oh, Finn, I killed him."

"No, you didn't," one of the men said. "He's out cold, but he'll just have a headache."

"Oh, thank goodness. I—Oh!" she gasped, as the lights came on.

"That's better," the man said. "Joe must have found the fuses. I'm Wheeler. Jared called and said there was trouble over here. We got here as soon as we could, but Miss Shaw obviously had everything under control."

"My father would not be a proud man," Finn said glumly.

"Hush, Finn," Liberty said. "How's your head?"

"It hurts. It's in as good a shape as my pride."

Wheeler laughed. "Lighten up on yourself, O'Casey. Every man does his own thing. I've seen some of your paintings. I'd trade in my gun tomorrow if

I could create what you do on canvas. Truth is, this line of work is all I know, all I'm cut out for."

" 'This above all: to thine own self be true,' " Liberty said.

"That's old Bill again," Finn said.

"I've got the other joker," Joe called from out front.

"Joe has Bo," Liberty said merrily. "That rhymes. Isn't that cute?"

"Liberty?" Finn said. "Are you getting flaky on me here?"

"Hmm?"

"Better give her a shot of something strong, O'Casey," Wheeler said. "I'd say reaction is setting in. We'll get these two out of your way, then call Jared and tell him it's wrapped up."

"He didn't happen to mention how his wife was, did he?" Finn asked.

"Oh, yeah, I nearly forgot. Tabor wasn't in an accident. Jared was conned, and he's fuming because he fell for it."

"I know the feeling," Finn said miserably.

"It can happen to anyone," Wheeler said. He hauled a moaning Mr. Manfield to his feet. "Bill the feds for your front door, Finn. At least it stopped raining. See ya. It was a pleasure meeting you, Miss Shaw."

"Thanks for everything," Finn said.

"Ta-ta," Liberty said, waggling her fingers.

"You definitely need a drink," Finn said to her as the other men left the house. "Come sit down."

He settled her onto the sofa, then brought her a drink. She swallowed it in one gulp, then shuddered.

"Blak," she said. "That's awful stuff."

"Well, it's bringing some color back to your cheeks. You were white as a ghost. Lord, you were really fantastic."

"How's your head now?"

"It'll be all right. I seem to be making a habit of getting whopped on the head. When I think of you being alone in this room with those two—"

"Finn, don't. It's finished. Do you realize that? The riddle is solved, the nightmare is over, we can get back to leading lives like normal people."

"That's true. We have a lot to talk about, Liberty, but right now we need some sleep. I'll find something to board up the broken door and window, then we're calling this day quits."

"You'll get no argument from me. I'm exhausted."

He stood up slowly. "Oh, my aching self. Do you want to hear a further confession? I was so groggy and out of it when I came staggering down that hall, I thought I heard someone call for Donder and Blitzen. I swear to heaven, Liberty, I'm not cut out to be an agent. I'm really not." He crossed the room and disappeared into the kitchen.

Liberty simply smiled.

Nine

Two days later, four newspapers rustled in the quiet room as the four people reading them turned the pages. There were several womanly gasps as well as a variety of earthly expletives. At last the papers were lowered and Liberty, Finn, Tabor, and Jared looked at one another.

"Unbelievable," Tabor said.

"It is incredible," Liberty said. "And it all happened because of Victoria Manfield's diary."

"She was remarkably careless with that," Jared said. "Can you imagine her writing down such incriminating information, and then just leaving it lying around her bedroom?"

"Obviously," Finn said, "she wasn't cut out to be a criminal. Do you realize how many people were arrested? Including the entire Manfield family."

"Hank did a helluva job," Jared said. "His agents were spread out all over the city and state, and there wasn't more than a thirty-second difference in timing in making the arrests. No one had an opportunity to warn anyone else to cut and run." He shook his head. "Me? I was eating fried shrimp in New Orleans."

"Now, now," Tabor said, patting his knee, "we all know how angry you and Finn are at yourselves. You're being very macho, sirs, but do notice that neither Liberty nor I are blaming you two." Mischief danced in Tabor's brown eyes. "After all, Liberty had things nicely under control here. She simple took change, creamed the bad guys, and—"

"Don't you have a plane to catch?" Finn interrupted gruffly.

"Finn, really," Liberty said, "you shouldn't be rude to your sister. Carry on, Tabor. You were saying?"

Jared laughed and got to his feet, extending his hand to Tabor. "We've met our match, Finn. I, for one, am slinking back to Vegas to heal my wounded male pride. Our plane awaits, my love," he said to Tabor. "We have to pick up Turtle and Crusher on the way to the airport. Crusher is retiring from the agency and is going to work at Miracles."

"They're so sweet together," Tabor said. "Oh, I hope they get married. And your aunt Beverly and Clarence," she went on, turning to Liberty. "They sound perfect for each other. And it's wonderful you'll be able to see them from time to time."

"Yes," Liberty said. "I'm looking forward to finally getting to know my aunt."

"Come on now, Tabor," Jared said.

Finn stood and kissed his sister on the cheek. "So long."

She smiled at him. "I'll talk to you soon, Finn. I didn't have a chance to get caught up on all the details of"—she glanced at Liberty—"your news."

"Go," Finn said, pointing to the front door.

"You're no fun," she said, then gave Liberty a hug. "I'm so glad you're here. 'Bye."

"Good-bye," Liberty said. "Good-bye, Jared."

"See y'all," Jared said. "We'll go out through the center door, Finn, since yours is boarded up. No need to come, I'll lock up behind us."

Waves and more good-byes were exchanged, then silence fell over Finn's large living room. He turned to see Liberty staring into the cold, empty hearth of the fireplace.

"Liberty?"

She looked at him. "Yes?"

"You seemed a million miles away just now."

"No," she said quietly, "not that far."

His jaw tightened. "Only as far as Chicago?"

She lifted her chin. "Yes, as a matter of fact, I *was* thinking about Chicago. There's nothing unusual about that. After all, I live there, my home is there. It's where . . . I belong." She cleared her throat. "I adore Tabor and Jared. They're really wonderful people, and anyone can see how happy—"

"Liberty, I love you."

"—they are together," she finished weakly. "What?"

He walked slowly over to her. He wove his fingers through her silky hair and looked directly into her eyes.

"I love you, Liberty Shaw. I'm asking you to be my wife, to share my life for all time."

Tears filled her eyes. "Oh, Finn, don't. You mustn't say that."

"Why not? It's true. I love you. Do you love *me*, Liberty?"

"I . . ."

"Do you?"

"Yes! Yes, I love you, Finn O'Casey, but . . ."

"Thank God." He stared up at the ceiling for a moment before looking at her again. "I've dreamed about hearing you say those words."

"No, no, it doesn't matter that I said them. It doesn't matter how I feel, or you feel. Nothing has changed, Finn. I thought we'd have the summer, our do-something-different time together, but now we can't even have that." Tears spilled onto her cheeks. "Would you take me to The Book Mark please?"

"No way." He dropped his hands from her hair and gripped her shoulders. "What is this garbage about it not mattering how we feel about each other? We love each other, dammit, and that matters a helluva lot. That's as big as it gets. I'm not talking about do-something-different time here, lady. This is forever, the rest of our lives."

"Finn, it's not that simple, don't you see? We come from different worlds and—"

"Liberty, you don't even like Chicago. I understand why you've stayed there, I really do. But we, you and me, together, are going to create our own place, a permanent place, just like you want and need."

"It's not Chicago. I'd leave there in a second,

break my contract, come to you, but—but there's no room for me here."

"You're not making any sense," he said, shaking his head.

"Let's go into your studio." She pulled out of his grasp and started across the room.

"Why?" he asked, not moving.

"Please," she said, quickening her step.

"Easy does it, O'Casey," Finn said under his breath. "Don't blow this."

When they reached the studio, Liberty walked to the center of the room, then turned to face Finn. She fought against the ache of tears in their throat.

"This," she said, "is your world. This is your first love, your mistress, where you belong. This studio is huge, but it's already overflowing with you, your talent, your hopes and dreams. There's no room for me, Finn."

"That's not true, Liberty. Dammit, that is *not* true. I've told you that I'm a man as well as an artist. And I've bared my soul to you, admitted that the man is lonely. I love you, and I also need you in my life."

"It won't work. You've devoted yourself to your painting. It's who you are, who you were meant to be. Your mistress will call your name in a voice louder than my whispers of love. And you'll go to her, to this room, because it's where you belong. A writer must write, a painter must paint. There's no middle road."

"Yes, there is. Okay, so I've put my art first for many years, but I don't have to do that anymore. I've made a name for myself, can have a normal balance in my life. It's the man's turn to be fulfilled, and I can only achieve that with you. I'll change my work schedule, Liberty, put in reasonable hours like any other husband and father. Don't you believe me?"

A sob caught in her throat. "I believe that *you* believe it, now, at this moment, as you're saying the words. But she'll call your name and you'll come, because you'll have no choice. That's the way it is, the way it has to be. And I'll be the one left alone and lonely."

"No!" He crossed the room and pulled her roughly into his arms, holding her to him as she buried her face in his chest. "No, it wouldn't be like that. My God, Liberty, you've got to give us a chance, give *me* a chance. We're talking about the rest of our lives, our happiness, everything we can have together. Don't throw all that away. I'm going to change, I swear it. We can have it all, don't you see that?"

"I . . . No . . . I don't know." Tears streamed down her face. "It's so big, your art, so powerful. It's like my father's army career. He was a soldier first, *then* a husband and father. He made so many promises that he couldn't keep because he had to go when they told him to. I learned not to count on him, not to believe he'd be there when he said he would so it wouldn't hurt so much. I can't live like that again, Finn. I just can't."

"Oh, Liberty, that's not how we'd live. Do you remember the quote I yelled through the door the night you told me to say something Finny so you'd know it was me? I said, 'I am the master of my fate; I am the captain of my soul.' Those words are true. *I* control my life. I'm not a marionette whose strings are pulled by a mistress named art. She isn't stronger than I am. I gave her many years, endless hours, and I don't regret that. But it's time for change. I'm ready, I need it. *I need you.* And, oh, God, Liberty, I love you so much."

"I love you too, Finn," she said, sobbing openly, "but I'm so afraid. I know exactly what I have in Chicago. It's there, it's real, permanent. The only promises I deal with are the ones I make to myself. You wouldn't intentionally hurt me, Finn, any more than my father did, but it happens when there's such a powerful force dictating to you. You have so much talent, so much to give, and the people, they're out there, wanting more, demanding more. It's all so frightening."

He was losing her, Finn thought incredulously, as panic rushed through him in an icy wave. He was holding her tightly in his arms, and he could virtually feel her slipping away from him, getting ready to run to her safe haven in Chicago. He didn't know what else to say, what words to use to convince her that the pain of her childhood wouldn't touch their love. Dammit, he couldn't, wouldn't, let her go. He couldn't lose his Liberty.

She lifted her head to look up at him. Her cheeks were streaked with tears. "Please take me back to The Book Mark now. I just—just can't talk anymore, or I'll cry for hours. Please?"

A flicker of pain crossed over his face. "All right," he said, his voice raspy. "But, Liberty, promise me that you'll think what I said. I'll give you time to sort it all through. I won't push you. Will you do that much at least?"

She nodded as she swiped at her tears. "Yes, I

promise I'll think about what you said, all of it. And about us, the fact that we love each other. But—"

"No," he interrupted, "don't say any more right now. Just keep your promise. I swear I won't rush you. I'll be here waiting for you. I won't come to The Book Mark and make you feel cornered or pressured. I love you, Liberty. I guess there's nothing more that I can say."

"I love you too," she whispered, but the words were muffled by a sob.

The drive to The Book Mark was made in total silence.

Liberty sat with her hands clutched tightly in her lap, willing no more tears to fall. She glanced once at Finn and saw the rigid set to his jaw, the pallor of his skin beneath his golden tan. His knuckles were white from his tight grip on the steering wheel.

She felt as though her heart were shattering into a million pieces.

At the store, he set her suitcases just inside the door and glanced at the books strewn in every direction on the floor.

"Manfield really did a number on this place," he said quietly. "I hate to leave you alone with this mess to tackle."

"I'll be fine," she said, looking at the middle of his chest. "Please go, Finn, because I'm about to start crying again, and I need to be alone right now."

"Yeah, okay." He lifted one hand and stroked his thumb over her tear-stained cheek. "See ya,

McGee," he said, his voice choked with emotion. He turned and left the store, closing the door behind him.

"See ya, Fletch," she said to the empty room. "Oh, God, Finn." She covered her face with her hands and wept.

The next morning, Liberty began to restore the apartment to order. The scene in Finn's studio ran constantly before her eyes like a nonstop movie, his words echoing over and over in her mind. Tears kept filling her eyes and she would angrily dash them away as she continued to work.

She was keeping her promise to Finn to think about all he had said, but no solution miraculously appeared, no light dawned at the end of the dark, lonely tunnel. She was in love with and loved by the wrong man.

By noon on the third day after returning to The Book Mark, the apartment was once again presentable. Liberty was tired from her labors, and from the restless nights spent tossing and turning and missing Finn.

She felt cut off from the world, held captive by her own tormented thoughts, and knew she had to escape for a while before starting to work on the disaster waiting for her below in the store.

She suddenly remembered that while she had been reading the newspaper at Finn's, she'd seen a boxed ad for the gallery that showed Finn's work. The ad had stated that while all of Finn O'Casey's work had been sold, the show would continue to run for the next week as previously announced.

Liberty showered and dressed in a white wrap-around skirt and a pale blue blouse. She realized as she brushed her hair that she didn't know why she felt such a driving need to go to that gallery, to see more of Finn's paintings. She only knew she had to go. Finn's mistress was calling her name.

She took a taxi to the gallery, then walked slowly into the large viewing room. She glanced at her brochure, which gave the name of each painting by number, but was unable to read it through the mist of tears in her eyes.

She moved from picture to picture, the ache in her heart growing more painful with each step she took.

Dear heaven, she thought, such talent Finn O'Casey possessed. What a rare, wonderful, special gift. There, on canvas, captured for eternity were unforgettable faces, quiet beach scenes, tempestuous storms, children, old people . . . *life*. Each one was different, and each one had been bought by someone who had felt a pull on his heartstrings when he'd seen it. This was Finn's world. This was where he belonged.

Liberty skirted a pillar and nearly bumped into a tiny, white-haired woman who was staring at a painting.

"I'm sorry," Liberty said. "I didn't see you."

The woman dabbed at her eyes with a lace-edged linen hankie. "It's my fault, dear. I'm afraid I become totally engrossed in my painting when I come to visit it."

Liberty looked up at the canvas. A weeping willow stood on the top of a gentle hill that was covered in a bright carpet of wild poppies.

"It's lovely," she said softly. "Very beautiful."

"Fifty years ago," the woman said, "my husband, my Bobby, proposed to me under a tree just like that one. I lost him to death six months ago. When I saw this painting the opening night of Mr. O'Casey's show, it was as though time had been turned back just for me and Bobby. I bought it, and will take it home soon where I can see it whenever I choose. These are not tears of sorrow I'm crying, dear, but of joy. I'd been wallowing in misery and loneliness ever since Bobby died. But when I saw this picture and remembered all the years of smiles, laughter, and love we'd shared, I realized I had been truly blessed. Finn O'Casey gave me back my Bobby. Oh, I must sound like a foolish old woman."

Unnoticed tears spilled onto Liberty's cheeks. "No, no, you don't sound foolish at all."

"Child, I've made you cry. What's wrong, my dear?"

"Nothing," Liberty said, smiling through her tears. "Thanks to you everything is, I hope, going to be just fine now." She gave the petite woman a quick hug. "Thank you so much, so very, very much."

Liberty ran from the gallery, leaving the woman staring at her with a bewildered expression on her face.

• • •

Finn tossed the soda can into the trash, then wandered into the living room. He should go into the studio, he supposed, and try, again, to paint. But no, not now. There was no point in it because he couldn't concentrate on his work, couldn't think about anything or anyone except Liberty. Lord, he missed her, ached for her, lived in chilling fear that she'd appear at his newly installed front door with the single purpose of saying good-bye forever.

He felt as though he were living in limbo, waiting for a verdict that was going to determine his entire future happiness. That, he thought ruefully, wasn't just how he felt. It was exactly the way things were.

He sighed and paced back and forth across the living room, wondering absently how long he could make his frequent trek without wearing out the carpet. He replayed in his mind, yet again, that final scene with Liberty in his studio, hearing her words and his, wishing he had said something different, better, something that would have kept her with him. But he'd spoken from his heart, his soul, and hadn't known what else to say. What was Liberty thinking now? In what direction was *her* heart and soul pulling her? Lord, he loved her so much.

The ringing of the doorbell brought him from his tormented thoughts, and he walked slowly across the room. A brief conversation with even a salesman would be a welcome respite from his jumbled, taunting thoughts, he decided.

He opened the door and heard the echo of his pounding heart in his ears.

"Liberty."

"Hello, Finn," she said quietly. He looked so

tired, she thought, but he was still beautiful. "May I come in?"

"Yes. Yes, of course," he said, stepping back. She was so lovely, he thought. So very lovely. He wanted to take her in his arms and . . . "Sit down," he said, closing the door.

Liberty crossed the room to the fireplace, then turned to look at him. He started toward her, then stopped halfway across the room. Their eyes met for a long moment, then Liberty tore her gaze from his and cleared her throat.

"There's something I have to say to you," she said, her voice trembling slightly.

Not good-bye, he screamed silently. Oh, please, Liberty, not good-bye. "All right."

"Finn, the things I said to you that day in your studio about your art coming first, being your demanding mistress, were true. I'm right about that, I know I am."

"But—"

"No, please, hear me out. I was also wrong about a great many things. Finn, today I went to the gallery where your paintings are being shown. I met a woman who told me why one of your paintings meant so much to her, how it had changed her life. Your gift has brought renewed joy to her, given her back something she felt she'd lost for all time. She's only one of a multitude who have been touched by your art."

She blinked back threatening tears. "It came to me then, Finn, as I spoke with that woman, the truth about myself. I was behaving like a child, a selfish, self-centered child. I wanted all your attention. I was always to come first, or I'd say it wasn't good enough. You were to be responsible for my happiness in the present and future, and also make up for the loneliness of my youth. I wouldn't share. Oh, no, not me. You were mine, and your art be damned. Since I knew your art was so very important to you, I ran. Crying my childish tears, I ran."

"Liberty, you're being too hard on yourself. I—"

She raised a hand to silence him, and saw that she was shaking.

"Finn, you aren't responsible for my happiness, past, present, or future. *I* am. It's up to me to be fulfilled within myself as a woman. I can't do that as a teacher because it isn't enough. It's too empty, too defeating. I continued to teach and live in Chicago because I didn't have the courage to leave. Well, now I do. I'm going to sell The Book Mark, but only the building. I'm keeping the books, and I'm going to find a bright, sunny place to open a new store. I'll have a special section for children, a corner where people can relax and read. It's going to be a wonderful store."

She took a deep steadying breath.

"And you will paint," she went on, "as you were meant to. If you come out of your studio at day's end in time to eat meat loaf, I'll be waiting. If you don't emerge for two days, I'll still be waiting. Waiting, Finn, with love and pride, knowing that what you are creating within that room is going to brighten the lives of others. Yes, I must share you with your mistress and the people beyond our door, but I'll be secure in the knowledge that our love is forever, is strong, real, and true enough to allow room for all the other things that make us who are we."

She gave up her battle against her tears, and they spilled onto her pale cheeks.

"Oh, Finn, I'm so sorry," she whispered. "Forgive me, please, for acting like a child, for allowing my insecurities and fears to blind me to the beauty of what we can have together. I love you, Finn, so very much. I want to be your wife, if you'll still have me. And you will paint, knowing that when the artist hears the voice of the man, I'll be waiting."

"Oh, God," Finn said, with a groan. "Oh, Liberty."

He closed the distance between them and pulled her to him, his mouth melting over hers. She filled her senses with the taste, and feel, and aroma of him as she answered the urgent demands of his lips and tongue. Her body hummed with joy, and her heart echoed the melody.

He finally lifted his head and looked directly into her eyes. "I love you so much," he said. "I was so afraid that you'd—No, forget that. You're here with me, you're home."

"Yes," she said, smiling through her tears, "I'm home. I came to you, Finn, and you were waiting, just as I'll wait for you when you're painting. We're going to have a wonderful life together."

His eyes were unusually bright as he smiled at her, weaving his fingers through her hair. "You bet we are, McGee." He kissed her again. "Lord, how I want you. I missed you terribly."

"I want you too," she said, pressing closer to his aroused body. "You want me and I want you. Have a solution to that riddle, Fletch?"

He swung her up into his arms. "I can handle this one, McGee, but it may take hours."

She circled his neck with her arms. "Oh, good. 'If you do not think about the future, you cannot have one.' "

"John Galsworthy," Finn said, starting across the room. "And we have one, together. There's only one thing about the future that disturbs me." He entered the bedroom and set her on her feet, holding her close. "I think we should discuss it now and get it out of the way."

She looked up at him anxiously. "What is it, Finn?"

A wide smile broke across his face. "I really hate meat loaf."

"Oh, I could strangle you, Fletch."

"Just love me, Liberty Shaw."

"I will love you forever, Finn O'Casey. And you may quote me on that."

Epilogue

Liberty came running in the front door, dropped her sweater and purse on a chair, and began to unbutton her blouse. Finn looked at her from where he sat on the sofa dressed in a suit and tie. He cocked an eyebrow as the blouse hit the floor and Liberty began to wiggle out of her skirt.

"I know I'm late . . . again," she said, nearly gasping for breath. "But, oh, Finn, this marvelous old man came into the bookstore. He had to be in his seventies, but his voice was rich and deep, and he began to read poetry aloud. People gathered, and we were mesmerized."

Finn watched the skirt join the blouse, followed by shoes, then a lacy slip. Liberty started skimming off her panty hose.

"I know we have reservations for dinner," she rushed on, "but I'll whiz through my shower and be dressed in a flash. Tell me you lost track of time, too, and painted longer than usual."

"Nope," he said, chuckling. "I put in my eight hours and quit."

"Darn, darn, darn. Not once in the six months that we've been married have you stayed in your studio past the schedule you set up. Me? I keep you waiting all the time."

He stood up, his heated gaze sweeping over her body, now clad only in a wispy bra and panties.

"Believe me, Mrs. O'Casey, you're worth waiting for."

"Why, thank you, Mr. O'Casey," she said, smiling at him.

He pulled off his tie and shrugged out of his jacket.

"What are you doing?" she asked. "What about our dinner reservations?"

"I've already called and changed them to later . . . much later." He pulled his shirt free of his pants.

She began to unfasten the buttons on his shirt. "I like the way your mind works, Fletch. Oh, Finn, I'm so happy, and I love you so much."

"I love you too, McGee," he said, laughing softly. "But I sure wish you'd solve the riddle of those buttons a little faster. This is Finn the man, not the artist, speaking."

She slid her hands over his bare chest. "And this is Liberty the woman, listening. Your woman, Finn, for now and always."

He sucked in his breath as her busy fingers began to work on his belt buckle.

"I have to make a phone call," he said, his voice strained.

"Now? To who?"

"It's 'whom,' and I'm canceling our reservations for dinner."

Liberty laughed in loving delight, then flung her arms around his neck and kissed him.

THE EDITOR'S CORNER

This coming month brings to mind lions and lambs—not only in terms of the weather, but also in terms of our six delightful LOVESWEPTs. You'll find fierce and feisty, tame and gentle characters in our books next month who add up to a rich and exciting array of folks whose stories of falling in love are enthralling.

First, hold on to your hat as a really hot wind blows through chilly London town in Fayrene Preston's marvelous *The Pearls of Sharah II: RAINE'S STORY*, LOVESWEPT #318. When Raine Bennett realized someone was following her through foggy Hyde Park one night, she ran . . . straight into the arms of Michael Carr. He was a stranger who radiated danger and mystery—yet he was a man Raine instinctively knew she could trust. Michael was utterly captivated by her, but the magnificent strand of perfect pearls draped across her exquisite body complicated things. What was she doing with the legendary Pearls of Sharah, which had just been reported stolen to his branch of Interpol? What were her secrets and would she threaten his integrity . . . as well as his heart? This is a dazzling love story you just can't let yourself miss! (Do remember that the Doubleday hardcover edition is available at the same time the paperback is in the stores. Don't miss this chance to collect all three Pearls of Sharah romances in these beautifully bound editions at only $12.95.)

Jan Hudson's **THE RIGHT MOVES**, LOVESWEPT #319, will set your senses ablaze. Jan created two unique characters in her heroine and hero; they were yin and yang, fire and ice, and they could not stay away from each other no matter how hard they tried. Chris Ponder was a spitfire, a dynamo with a temper . . . and with a tow truck. When she took one look at Nick Russo's bedroom eyes, her insides turned to tapioca, and she suddenly wanted to flirt with the danger he represented. But good sense started to prevail. After all, she hardly needed to fall for a handsome charmer who might be all flash and no substance. Still Nick teased, and she felt she might go up in flames . . . especially on one moonlit night that filled her with wonder. This is a breathlessly exciting romance!

In LOVESWEPT #320, **THE SILVER BULLET AFFAIR**, Sandra Chastain shows us once again that love sure can conquer all. When John Garmon learned that his brother Jeffrey's will instructed him to "Take care of Caitlan and the

(continued)

baby—it's mine," he immediately sought out the quicksilver lady who had charmed him at every former meeting. Caitlan proved to be like a fine perfume—good at disappearing and very elusive. She believed that John was her adversary, a villain, perhaps, who might take her baby away if he learned the truth. So how could she lose herself in the hot shivery sensations of his embrace? Bewitched by this fragile woman who broke all the rules, John grows determined to rescue Caitlan from her free-spirited life and the gang of crazy but caring friends who never leave them alone to learn to love each other. A shimmering, vivid love story that we think you'll find a real delight.

The brilliant . . . fun . . . thrilling . . . surprising conclusion to the "Hagen Strikes Again" series, by Kay Hooper, **ACES HIGH,** LOVESWEPT #321, comes your way next month. Skye Prescott was tall, dark, and dangerous, a man who'd never forgotten how Katrina Keller had betrayed him years before. In a world where survival depended on suspicion, he'd fallen in love—and it had broken him as violence never had. When the beautiful redheaded ghost from his past reappeared in his life, Skye was filled with fury, hurt, a desire for revenge—and an aching hunger to make Katrina burn for him again. Katrina had fought her memories, but once she was in his arms, she couldn't fight him or her own primal passion. She was his match, his mate—but belonging to him body and spirit gave him the power to destroy her. When Skye faced his most violent enemy, Trina knew she faced the most desperate gamble of her life. Now, friends, need I tease you with the fact that Hagen also gets his in this fabulous book? I know you've been wondering (as all of us here have) what Kay was going to do for that paunchy devil in terms of a love story. Well, next month you will know. And I can guarantee that Kay has been as delightfully inventive as we had hoped and dreamed she would be.

Please give a great, warm welcome to talented new author Marcia Evanick by getting and enjoying her powerfully emotional romance, **PERFECT MORNING,** LOVESWEPT #322. How this story will touch your heart! When Jason Nesbit entered Riki McCormick's front yard in search of his young daughter, he never expected to find an emerald-eyed vixen as her foster mother. He had just learned that he had a child when his ex-wife died in an accident. Traumatized after her mother's death, the girl had not spoken since. Jason marveled at Riki's houseful of love—and was capti-

(continued)

vated by the sweet, spirited woman who'd made room in her life for so many special children. Under Jason's steamy scrutiny, Riki felt a wave of longing to be kissed breathless and held tight. When his Texas drawl warned her that her waiting days were over, she unpacked her slinkiest lingerie and dreamed of satin sheets and firelight. But courting Riki with seven children around seemed downright impossible. You'll laugh and cry with Jason and Riki as they try to make everyone happy. A keeper!

Halsey Morgan is alive—and Stevie Lee wanted him dead. What a way to open a romance! Glenna McReynolds has created two wonderful, thrilling characters in LOVESWEPT #323, **STEVIE LEE.** Halsey Morgan was Stevie Lee's long-lost neighbor. She had plotted for the last few years to buy his cabin for his back taxes, sell it for a huge profit, and get out of her small town so she could see the world. Handsome Halsey had blazed a trail of adventure from the Himalayas to the Amazon—and was thought to be dead. Now he was back—ruining her plans to escape and melting her with sizzling kisses that almost made her forget why she'd ever wanted to go away. His wildness excited her senses to riot, while his husky voice made her tremble with want. Hal had never stayed anywhere long enough to fall in love, but Stevie was the answer to a loneliness he'd never dared admit. He made her take chances, climb mountains, and taught her how to love him. But could Hal persuade her to risk loving him and follow her dreams while held tight in his arms? Don't miss this great story . . . which, we think you'll agree, knocks your socks off!

Enjoy those blustery days next month curled up with six LOVESWEPTs that are as hot as they are happily-ever-after.

Carolyn Nichols

Carolyn Nichols
Editor
LOVESWEPT
Bantam Books
666 Fifth Avenue
New York, NY 10103